W9-CGZ-375

This marriage ploy was purely a business arrangement.

So why this sudden, wild desire to make their pact anything *but* pure?

"Money can't buy happiness, Mr. Dragan!"

"But money lets you look for happiness in a lot of nice places."

A chill dashed down Trisha's spine. Suddenly the idea of spending two weeks with the luscious Lassiter Dragan became a disgraceful travesty. From the first instant she'd met him she'd been drawn to the man. But the fairy tale had dissolved, disappeared, and she mentally hauled out all her defenses.

She wouldn't walk out on their deal. But any crazy illusions Trisha might have had about The Gentleman Dragon being a modern-day Prince Charming had to be stomped to dust.

Renee Roszel has been writing romance novels since 1983 and simply loves her job. She likes to keep her stories humorous and light, with her heroes gorgeous, sexy and larger than life. She says, "Why not spend your days and nights with the very best!" Luckily for Renee, her husband is gorgeous and sexy, too!

Renee Roszel loves to hear from her readers. Send your letter and SASE to P.O. Box 700154, Tulsa, Oklahoma 74170 U.S.A. Or visit her Web site at www.ReneeRoszel.com.

Don't miss any of our special offers. Write to us at the following address for information on our newest releases.

Harlequin Reader Service
U.S.: 3010 Walden Ave., P.O. Box 1325, Buffalo, NY 14269
Canadian: P.O. Box 609, Fort Erie, Ont. L2A 5X3

A BRIDE
FOR THE HOLIDAYS
Renee Roszel

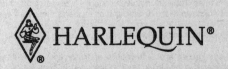

HARLEQUIN®

TORONTO • NEW YORK • LONDON
AMSTERDAM • PARIS • SYDNEY • HAMBURG
STOCKHOLM • ATHENS • TOKYO • MILAN • MADRID
PRAGUE • WARSAW • BUDAPEST • AUCKLAND

If you purchased this book without a cover you should be aware
that this book is stolen property. It was reported as "unsold and
destroyed" to the publisher, and neither the author nor the
publisher has received any payment for this "stripped book."

To animal rescue societies that take in the broken,
abused and abandoned four-legged angels among us.
Adopt a dog or cat.
Give yourself the gift of unconditional love.

ISBN 0-373-03778-3

A BRIDE FOR THE HOLIDAYS

First North American Publication 2003.

Copyright © 2003 by Renee Roszel Wilson.

All rights reserved. Except for use in any review, the reproduction or
utilization of this work in whole or in part in any form by any electronic,
mechanical or other means, now known or hereafter invented, including
xerography, photocopying and recording, or in any information storage
or retrieval system, is forbidden without the written permission of the
publisher, Harlequin Enterprises Limited, 225 Duncan Mill Road,
Don Mills, Ontario, Canada M3B 3K9.

All characters in this book have no existence outside the imagination of
the author and have no relation whatsoever to anyone bearing the same
name or names. They are not even distantly inspired by any individual
known or unknown to the author, and all incidents are pure invention.

This edition published by arrangement with Harlequin Books S.A.

® and TM are trademarks of the publisher. Trademarks indicated with
® are registered in the United States Patent and Trademark Office, the
Canadian Trade Marks Office and in other countries.

Visit us at www.eHarlequin.com

Printed in U.S.A.

CHAPTER ONE

THE ringing phone blasted through the stillness of the empty coffee shop like a tornado siren. Trisha's breath caught and froze in her chest. She instinctively knew this was the call she'd been waiting for.

Her last chance.

The polished aluminum and white-tiled surroundings evaporated from her consciousness as she vaulted over the mop bucket part-time employee, Amber Grace, had dragged out to clean up a spilled latte.

Trisha grabbed the wall phone's receiver, fumbling, almost dropping it before she managed a firm enough grasp to lift it to her ear. "Ed's Gourmet Java Joint." She swallowed, forcing the nervous quiver from her voice. "Trisha August, Day Manager, speaking."

She recognized the caller's voice—the bank loan officer, telephoning with his verdict. Her heart pounded so furiously she could hardly hear over its deafening beat. This was her moment of truth—whether she would get her small business loan, or not.

Caught between wrenching anxiety and frothy optimism, she listened, nodded, hardly able to squeeze in more than a brief "yes" or "no" as the loan officer talked in a tone that was mincingly polite but distant.

Her heart sank. She'd heard that same thumbs-down speech so many times she couldn't stand hearing it again. "But, I'm very responsible and I'm a hard worker. I'll do anything for a loan!" she blurted, interrupting the lecture she knew was about to end in "Thank you for your interest in Kansas City Unified Bank." "I'll do anything you ask!" she cried. "*Please,* just give me a chance!"

Without even the courtesy of a pause to pretend he gave

her plea some thought, the loan officer delivered his "Thank you for your interest" line and hung up.

Trisha stood there with the receiver clenched in a fist. Raw anger at the unfairness of the world overwhelmed her. She could do this! She could make a success of herself, if somebody would only give her a chance! Her throat aching with fury, she slammed the receiver on its hook. "You can't borrow money if you don't have money!" Frustration and resentment coloring her words, she twisted away from the phone. "How does *anybody* ever open a business?"

"That's a good question," came a male voice. The comment had been spoken softly, the tone rich and deep and stirringly masculine.

Startled that a customer had entered without her notice, Trisha's gaze shot to the serving counter. A man stood there. A tall man, clad in a camel overcoat that Trisha guessed was made of the finest cashmere. His broad, expensively garbed shoulders twinkled with melting snow. Dark hair glittered, too. As fetching as all that sparkling and twinkling was in a fluorescent glare that didn't ordinarily show anyone to advantage, her attention was captured by his face.

What a face! He wasn't smiling, but a slight upturn at one side of his mouth, gave the impression of cavalier nonchalance. His lips were nice, wholly masculine without the exotic plumpness of some male models.

His eyes were sharp and assessing. That was obvious, even half masked beneath the long, thick sweep of his lashes. It was difficult to tell what color his eyes were, shadowed by such a sexy canopy. Brown, possibly gray.

Her hesitation must have been overlong, because the stranger with the scintillating eyes cleared his throat. "I'd like a cup of coffee."

Trisha felt like a fool. What had gotten into her? She stepped around Amber Grace and her mop, noticing belatedly that the teenager had also gone stock-still. In an aside, she murmured, "That latte isn't going to mop itself."

The teen blinked, coming back from never-never land. "Oh—yeah." Her mop began to move.

Trisha hurried to the counter and smiled, though the pleasant expression felt strained. That business loan would have helped her achieve her dream—and it was gone. She hadn't begun to deal with the bitter and unjust defeat, but she shoved the pain and outrage to a back shelf in her brain. This was neither the time nor place to vent her spleen. "Good afternoon, sir," she said as pleasantly as she could. "We have three special blends today, raspberry-vanilla, Jamaica-chocolate and orange—"

"Do you have anything called coffee?"

She could see his eyes better across the counter. They were gray. Steel gray. An unusual color, and attractive, yet a little too piercing for comfort.

For some bizarre reason she had trouble remembering if they had anything called coffee. Working to get her brain on track, she responded, "Uh—how about our Colombian Dark Secret?"

"As long as the dark secret is that it has coffee in it."

She found herself smiling, an amazing feat, considering her future had just been crushed under the unfeeling boot heel of corporate banking. "I promise it has coffee in it, sir," she said, still smiling in spite of her broken dreams. "What size would you like, biggie, biggie-extra or biggie-boggle?" As she named the sizes, she pointed out the small, medium and large cups affixed to the top of the latte machine.

"Medium," he said.

For some reason she liked that about him. He was a no-nonsense man who called a spade a spade. No fancy pseudo-speak cluttered his world. Just bare-boned facts. "Yes, sir." She moved away to retrieve a cup and pour him a medium order of strong, black coffee. And he would drink it black, she knew. Black, strong and unadulterated. A real man's cup of coffee.

A real man's cup of coffee? What a silly, fanciful thought to have about a total stranger. She shook it off.

Her back to him, she sidled to the Colombian Dark Secret spigot and pulled the lever. Funny, she could feel his gaze on her. Not that lots of customers didn't follow her movements as she got their order, but there was something different in the way she sensed his gaze. Her cheeks grew hot and she felt a tremor of feminine excitement, to think such a man might—

"What is this business you can't get a loan for?"

She was so startled by his question she almost dropped the paper cup. When she regained her grip on it and opened the spigot again, she glanced over her shoulder. "Oh—I'm sorry you heard that, sir. I didn't mean to…" Now the heat in her cheeks was due to humiliation. How unprofessional of her to rant about her bad luck in front of a customer!

"No, tell me," he said, looking completely serious. "I might know somewhere you can go for that loan."

With the full cup of coffee, she returned to the counter. "I don't think so, sir," she said, shaking her head. "I've tried every place in town, plus everything on the Internet I can find." She indicated the cup lids in a cubbyhole beside others containing sugar and creamer packets, as well as red plastic stirrers. When he shook his head to decline, she held the cup toward him. "The only companies that would lend me money charged loan-shark interest rates."

"That's too bad." He reached for the coffee cup.

Just as he was about to take it, Trisha felt a sharp jab between her shoulder blades, hard enough to knock her off balance. She pitched forward, her forearms coming into explosive contact with the coffee bar's brushed aluminum countertop. She winced at the pain. "*Ouch!* What in the world…" Struggling up, she reached back to rub the throbbing spot where she'd been jabbed.

"Oops. What'd I hit?" Amber Grace asked in the nasal whine she used when she perpetrated one of her many crimes of incompetence. She turned around to face her boss. "Was it your back?"

Trisha stared at the young girl, reining in her temper with difficulty. *"You think?"*

Amber Grace wore her usual sheepish "lucky-I'm-Ed's-niece" face, but an instant later her expression changed to horror. "Oh!" She let go of the mop with one hand and pointed. "Look what *you* did to that man!"

Look what you did to that man!

Those seven dreadful words exploded in Trisha's head like gunfire. She didn't have to look to know his expensive cashmere coat was drenched with Colombian Dark Secret. A mortified sound issued up from her throat, a strangled expression of her grief at the loss of this week's paycheck. That's what it would cost her to get his coat cleaned. With great reluctance and even greater regret she faced the man in dripping cashmere.

His attention had dropped to the front of his coat. When their eyes met, his expression was not one of great cheer. "On second thought, a lid might have been a good idea."

"Oh, heavens!" Trisha would have given her right arm to take back the last few seconds. "I'm *so* sorry!"

"Napkins?" he asked, holding out the same hand that had almost secured the cup a moment before.

"Oh—of course!" She grabbed a stack from beneath the counter. Ed was stingy with his precious, printed napkins, insisting each customer get only one. But this was an emergency. "Amber Grace, run and grab some paper towels out of the back." She pressed an inch thick batch of napkins against the man's coatfront, mopping coffee from the material. Knowing Ed, she would have to pay for the napkins, too.

"I can't apologize enough, sir!" She flipped the batch of napkins to find fresh areas to absorb the spill. Sponging the man, she noticed there wasn't a marshmallowy inch on his entire abdomen. He must have a washboard gut under all that expensive fabric. Even steeped in self-contempt and dismay she experienced a rush of feminine admiration. "I really must insist that you let me clean your stomach!" she said.

His hands covered hers, removing the napkins from her fingers and taking over the job. "That's not necessary," he said, sounding less put-out than she would have imagined. "I think my stomach escaped most of the coffee."

Her gaze shot to his face. Had she actually offered to clean his *stomach?* Shamed to the soles of her feet, she cried, "Oh— I—I meant—your coat! I'd like to have your coat dry-cleaned, at my expense. It's the least—"

"Just fix me another cup of coffee," he said. "Forget the coat."

She swallowed around the lump of wretchedness in her throat. In the five months she'd worked at Ed's, she'd never spilled coffee on a single customer. And now, to spill a whole biggie-extra on this—this—gorgeous man—er—*coat!* And then, to make matters a thousand times worse, to offer to clean his *stomach!*

She found herself staring into his sexy but oh-so-steely gaze, mesmerized. Looking into those eyes, she experienced a strange contradiction within her. His gaze was all business and bottom-line, yet there was something compelling and exciting in the way he was able to hold her attention, something she couldn't name. But it was there, stunning and impossible to resist. Unnerved, she realized she'd lost her train of thought. "Er—excuse me?"

He laid the soaked stack of napkins on the coffee-doused countertop and accepted the roll of paper towels from a breathless Amber Grace. "Thank you," he said, tearing off a wad and applying it to his lapel. Odd, Trisha couldn't recall his gaze leaving hers. "I said, why don't you fix me another cup of coffee and forget the coat?"

"Oh—right." Trisha was so flustered and miserable she wasn't thinking clearly. *Take a breath,* she berated inwardly. *Calm down or you'll make things worse—if that's even possible!*

"Amber Grace?"

Trisha was surprised to hear the stranger speak directly to Ed's niece, and peered at them over her shoulder as she retrieved another cup.

"Yes, sir?" Amber Grace asked, an unusually dopey smile on her freckled face.

He handed her the roll of paper towels. "Why don't you wipe up the countertop?"

"Okay." The teenager's smile remained dopey and her gaze stayed on the stranger as she slowly unwound some of the towels and began to dab them on the wet counter.

Trisha turned away to fill the coffee cup, frustrated beyond words. There was no debating the fact that they would never see this customer again. Between her unprofessional rant about the loan, and Amber Grace's ineptitude, his impression of Ed's employees had to be pretty awful. And that wasn't taking into account the fact that she'd flung coffee all over him! She refused to even *think* about the—the stomach thing. Since he was kind enough to forget it, she would, too.

Someday, in the far, far distant future.

The stranger's languid-lidded eyes seemed to have a unique effect on females. Both she and Amber Grace were doing a first-class job of making idiots out of themselves. She wondered if this man sent all women into tizzies, or if she could possibly blame her bizarre behavior on a leak of laughing gas from the dentist's office next door? No. That was too much to hope for. They'd all be affected, and so far, the man with the great lips and bedroom eyes had only half smiled when he'd first come in. Since the spill, he hadn't smiled at all.

From the sappy look she'd seen on Amber Grace's face, the teenager was clearly gaga about the handsome stranger. Having made a complete fool of herself, Trisha couldn't very well blame Amber Grace for her infatuation. Unfortunately, it wouldn't do Amber Grace's industriousness any good, if her inattentive dabbing at the countertop was any indication.

Trisha filled the cup, returned to the counter and held it out to him, sternly telling herself to be all-business, and guard every single syllable that came out of her mouth. "Compliments of Ed's, sir," she said, not caring if she did have to pay for it herself. There was no way she would ask the man for three dollars and ninety-nine cents now. "You've been very gracious." She decided she must make her coat-cleaning offer once more. "I really would be happy to pay for having that beautiful coat dry-cleaned."

"It wasn't your fault." He accepted the cup, which was far less dangerous this time, since Amber Grace had suspended her wiping duties to rest her elbows on the damp countertop. Her chin plunked on her fists, she grinned dreamily at the man.

He took a sip of coffee, then seemed to savor it. "Not bad," he said. "I think it does have coffee in it."

Trisha was amazed that she was once again smiling. After all that had happened, she could only call it a miracle—or an act of a person who'd gone completely insane with disgrace and defeat. Looking at his chiseled features, those seductive, silvery eyes, and most especially that lopsided, casual quirk of his lips, she decided she had to go with "miracle." She'd never met a man before, who could shift his lips slightly, the way this stranger did, and sire an actual smile. Especially on her lips, that only moments ago she'd thought incapable of waywardness.

"Now, tell me about that business," he said.

She was startled by the suggestion. She'd assumed he'd asked to be polite. She couldn't imagine he truly cared. "Oh, I wouldn't want to bore you," she said.

He took another sip of coffee. "If you really want something, you should never pass up a chance to go after it."

He had a point. So what if she caused a stranger a little boredom compared to a shot at getting her life's dream?

"Go on, tell him," Amber Grace urged, her voice the rapt singsong of the hypnotized.

They both glanced at the loafing teenager, an outrageous riot of quarreling colors. Amber Grace was a sight to behold in a lemon yellow polo shirt, aqua trousers, topped by a ridiculous aqua cap, reminiscent of something a nineteen-fifties nurse might have worn. Her short, shaggy catsup-red hair was the consistency of straw, and her two golden nose rings gleamed under the glare of the lights. Amber Grace was the poster child for parental suffering, not to mention a Day Manager's nightmare.

The horrible uniform colors weren't Amber Grace's fault, though. They were Ed's. The ultra-frugal coffee shop owner had bought them on the Internet. Trisha suspected it had been during a "we can't get rid of these terrible uniforms" sale. But Ed was not only frugal, he was shrewd. He got his money back, probably made money, since he required his employees to buy their uniforms from him.

Except for the catsup-colored hair and the nose rings, Trisha knew she looked every bit as bad as Amber Grace. Who on earth looked good in yellow and aqua under stark fluorescent lights?

The ugliness of the uniforms hadn't really hit home until— well, until just this minute, when she realized how tacky she must look to this obviously discerning stranger, whose attire was so classic and tastefully elegant. *And coffee stained,* a nagging imp in her brain insisted on needling.

Trying not to dwell on things that couldn't be helped, Trisha plucked up the abandoned roll of paper towels and tore off a bunch. The man wanted to hear about her business, so she would be wise to get focused where she might do herself some good. "Well…" As she began to sop up spilled coffee, she chanced a peek at him to gauge his expression. His eyes were not glazed over, which was more than she could say for Amber Grace's.

"What I have in mind is a doggie boutique," she began, "where people can come to self-groom their pets—use my equipment, tubs, clippers et cetera, to bathe and spruce them up, for a highly reduced price from what a professional groomer would charge. And they'd leave the clipped hair, dirty bath water, splashed floor, in other words—the mess—behind."

Trisha had made her spiel a million times in the past five months, so she could tell it without thinking, which was lucky, since there was something about this man that made her thinking processes go fuzzy. "I've seen similar places. One in Wichita and one in Olathe. Both were doing business hand-over-fist. The customers love it. I know my shop would be a success here in Kansas City. I've found a vacant store in a strip center that's for rent. With a twenty-five thousand dollar loan and a lot of elbow grease I can fix it up really nice. I even have a great name for it—'Dog Days of August.'"

"Interesting name," he said, drawing her gaze in time to see a quizzical lift of his brow.

"It's really a great play on words because that's my name," she explained, returning her focus to her scrubbing. His eyes were hard to look into and think about anything but how sexy they were. She cleared her throat. "August. Trisha August."

She sighed long and low, expelling some of the frustration that had built up over months of rejections. "The only trouble is, I can't get financing. I've worked lots of jobs over the years, at several grooming places, too, so I know all about them. The last one I worked at closed when the owner retired, so I had to take this job."

She tossed the wet clump of towels in the trash and faced him, her expression as serious as her determination. "I've saved every cent I can, and I don't mind working long, hard hours to make my dream come true," she said. "But all the banks and loan companies give me the same speech—tired platitudes about how small businesses are very chancy, with so many failing in the first year. How banks can't operate without strict rules. About the importance of collateral and how I'm young, have no assets, little previous business experience and on and on and on," she cried. "Banks don't care how hard I'd work. They only care that I'm young and poor!" Her anger surged. "I'm not that young! I'm twenty-eight. I've been making it on my own since I was eighteen! And if I weren't *poor* I wouldn't need a loan!"

She slapped the flats of her hands to the countertop and leaned forward, feeling spent and worn down. "That call you heard was my last hope."

A shape moved in the corner of her eye and she shifted her attention to the shop's door. A man in a navy uniform of some kind had entered. He wore a navy, airline pilot style hat, though there was no gold braid on it. Snow sparkled on his dark clothes. In a military-like fashion he removed his cap and clasped it under one arm to stand at attention. He was nice looking, in his mid-twenties and muscular. Trisha noticed he also had on matching navy leather gloves and boots. "Sir," he said, "The flat has been repaired. If you're ready?"

The handsome customer who'd been listening to her business plan, shifted toward the newcomer and nodded. "Thank you, Jeffery. I'll be right out."

"Certainly, sir."

Outside Ed's plate glass window, Trisha noticed snow highlighted in the amber glow of a streetlamp. It was barely four-thirty and already dark. The rhythm and choreography of the snowfall had not changed all afternoon. There had to be a foot on the ground by now. Though it was only December eighteenth, with all the cold and snow they'd had this month, Kansas City had a real chance of having a white Christmas this year.

The man in navy departed with military bearing, leaving in his wake a dusting of quickly melting snow. Before Trisha could offer the handsome customer her abject apologies one last time, he picked up a napkin off a small stack that hadn't been used to sop coffee, leaned down and began to jot something on the back of it. "Your idea sounds solid, Miss August," he said, his golden pen flashing in the florescence as he wrote. "Make an appointment with this man. His office is in the Dragan building. Tell him what you told me." He straightened and handed her the napkin. "I think he'll help you."

Trisha accepted the napkin, confused. "The Dragan building?" she echoed.

He nodded, depositing his pen in an inside coat pocket. "Tell him Gent sent you."

"Gent—okay." She didn't know there were any banks or loan companies in the Dragan building. "What floor? What's the company's name?" She was surprised at her voice. She sounded a little panicky. She knew he was leaving, and she didn't want him to go. She didn't like the idea of never looking into those unusual eyes, ever again.

"Security will direct you," he said, turning away.

Bewildered, she stared down at the napkin. What had he said? Something about security directing her somewhere? Yeah, she'd just bet—right back out onto the street. She felt agitated, conflicted. She thought she believed him. She wanted to, but she wasn't sure she could. "Are you serious, Mr. Gent?" she asked.

When she got no answer, she pulled her gaze from the napkin. The stranger was gone—as quickly and as silently as he'd come. She dropped her attention back to the napkin, hoping against hope it was true. In bold script the man in cashmere had written "Herman Hodges, Dragan VC." Then he'd apparently signed it, since the only other word scrawled on the page looked like "Gent."

She wondered if this coffee-spotted paper napkin could actually hold the key to her dream. "Wow," she whispered, experiencing a flicker of hope. To think that this flimsy scrap of paper might be her passport to success was too astonishing to completely penetrate.

"Huh?"

Amber Grace stirred, belatedly coming out of her trance.

"Nothing." Trisha slowly shook her head, afraid to hope but unable to help herself. Gingerly folding the napkin, she slipped it in her trouser pocket. Even if it came to nothing, she had to try.

Like Mr. Gent said, *"If you really want something, you should never pass up the chance to go for it!"*

CHAPTER TWO

TRISHA sat stiffly in Herman Hodges' office, on the fiftieth floor of the Dragan building. Perched on the edge of her chair, she tried to hide her nervous anxiety, but she wanted desperately to go to the window and look at the snow fluttering down on the brick, glass and steel cityscape. Watching snow falling calmed her, and if she ever needed calming, she needed it now. Her fingers clamped around her handbag, she gamely faced the sixtyish, bald and portly, upper-management type as he leafed through her thin business file.

The folder contained her meticulously worked out doggie boutique plans. Her meager financial statement was also in that folder. It included one savings account that contained two thousand, three-hundred and ninety one dollars and eighty-seven cents, every penny she'd saved for the past decade. With no other assets, not even a car, Trisha wasn't encouraged by the expression on his face. Clearly he was wondering why in the world she was even there.

When Mr. Gent had suggested she meet with Mr. Hodges he'd told her the man was in the Dragan building, but she'd never suspected he was associated with Dragan Venture Capital Inc. She'd heard of the firm, but she never imagined they would deal in such paltry sums as the twenty-five thousand she wanted to borrow, though it was far from paltry to her.

She'd assumed Dragan Venture Capital dealt with high rollers who borrowed millions. Nonetheless, even as the nice security person had escorted her to the plush, fiftieth floor headquarters of Dragan Venture Capital, she refused to panic and run. The handsome stranger's words kept ringing in her head like a rallying cry.

"If you really want something, you should never pass up the chance to go for it!"

Witnessing Mr. Hodges' crinkled brow as he closed her file and lifted his attention from it, Trisha's "go for it" determination faltered. She could almost see the "Thank you for your interest" sentence forming on his lips. Working to hold on to her positive outlook, she cleared her throat and sat straighter in the cushy leather chair, opposite Mr. Hodges' polished oak desk.

"Well, Miss August," he began, his smile polite but not particularly warm. "I can see that you've put a lot of thought and effort into your—uh…" He paused, as though trying to recall what exactly she'd put a lot of thought into.

"Dog Days of August," she said, grateful her voice didn't squeak or break altogether.

"Right," he said, his pasted-on smile of looming rejection all too familiar. "Dog Days of August. A very clever name."

She held to her pleasant expression, clung to hope, though she felt like she was grasping a rock cliff with nothing but her fingernails between salvation and a plunge into oblivion.

He sat back and folded his hands over her file folder. He looked very successful and authoritative, lounging in his huge, tufted leather executive chair, dressed in an expensive charcoal suit, crisp white shirt and black, olive-green and purple paisley tie. She noticed his fingernails glimmered slightly. Good grief, the man's nails were professionally manicured. She felt awkward, uncomfortable. Even wearing her very best emerald green, wool suit and in freshly shined black pumps, her nails weren't as precisely groomed as this middle-aged man's. Now it was her turn to question why in the world she was here?

"You see, Miss August," he began, unmistakably going into lecture mode. She bit the inside of her cheek, a reflex reaction to threatening doom. "Dragan Ventures is an international company, our focus is on initiatives that can quickly dominate emerging, high-growth markets, and show a strong potential for delivering a ten to twenty times return on our investment within five to eight years, via an IPO or merger. Our target investment areas are communications infrastructure, business software technologies, semiconductor products, and new industrial technologies. Building on a strong technical and operational foundation, Dragan invests in the areas where we can contribute the highest degree of expertise and value.''

He paused, and Trisha had a scary feeling he expected her to respond. She had hardly understood a word he'd uttered, but she nodded. ''I see.'' She was fairly sure he suspected she didn't.

He leaned forward and she wondered if the move was to intimidate, as if he needed to work at it! ''To be frank, Miss August, even if we considered yours a good business risk, and even if we invested in—er—dog grooming parlors, our minimum investment is five million dollars. Twenty-five thousand is well under our radar, so to speak.'' He refreshed his smile, though it was neither warmer nor friendlier. ''Have you tried your local bank?''

A surge of bitter frustration rushed through her, and she fought the urge to roll her eyes at the condescension of his question. And she'd taken a sick day from work for this! ''Yes, sir, I have,'' she said, amazingly evenly, her white-knuckled hold on her handbag the only outlet she allowed herself for her emotional upset.

He lifted her file and leaned across the desk, offering it to her. ''Thank you for your interest in Dragan Venture Capital, Miss August, however, as I hope I made clear, we really aren't in the business of—''

''Yes, well,'' she said, cutting off the horrible rejection cliché she'd already heard too many times. ''I—I didn't think you were involved in ventures like mine, but when Mr. Gent suggested I see you, I thought—well, I *hoped*—he—''

''Mr. Who?''

Trisha took hold of her file, but when she tried to pull it from his fingers, she felt resistance and was confused. ''Excuse me?''

''*Who* did you say suggested that you see me?''

For the first time since Trisha set foot inside Mr. Hodges' expensively appointed office his eyes held a sentiment besides cool indifference. He actually seemed interested. Since he was strangely reluctant to release her file, she let go. "Mr. Gent," she repeated.

He eyed her suspiciously, unmoving. She wondered what was going through his mind. Whatever his thoughts, they weren't cheerful. She didn't enjoy feeling like a bug about to be squashed and decided to try and explain. "I—I assumed Mr. Gent was a client of yours. He acted as though you might want to help me."

Mr. Hodges eyes narrowed. "Are you saying this man's name is *Mr.* Gent?"

Trisha didn't know what she'd said to make Mr. Hodges so agitated. Who was this Mr. Gent, anyway? Had he defrauded Dragan Venture Capital, or defaulted on a loan? Was he some kind of con artist?

A thought struck like a two-by-four, shaking her to her core. *Heavens above!* Had Mr. Gent's suggestion that she go to Dragan Ventures been a cruel payback for staining his coat? Was he out there somewhere laughing his head off? Did a conniving sadist lurk beneath that handsome face? Well, why not? What was the cliché? "You can't tell a book by its cover." Clichés were born from long-standing, proven truths.

Sick to her stomach, and wanting to clear up this awful mess and get out as quickly as possible, she opened her square, black handbag and pulled out the napkin. "He didn't tell me his name. He wrote it down, though. I—I'll show you." Her heart sank further just looking at the coffee spattered thing. How could she have been so gullible to believe such an obvious *prank?* She felt ridiculous handing him the piece of absorbent paper, and couldn't quite meet his narrowed gaze.

He took the limp, wrinkled napkin from her fingers and frowned at it.

The quiet was so ominous, Trisha had to fill it with either a scream or a defense. Working at remaining at least outwardly composed, she opted for the defense. "You see, a man—a customer at the coffee shop where I work—asked me about my doggie boutique idea. He acted like he thought it had potential, wrote your name on this napkin and told me to come see you. Naturally, I should have realized it was too good to—''

"Would you excuse me for a moment, Miss August?"

Trisha was caught with her mouth open, startled by his troubled tone and the suddenness of his rise from his chair. She didn't think such a beefy man could move that quickly. "Why—uh—certainly…" Her sentence died away as the man dashed out a side door. She stared after him, her unease becoming unreasoning fear. What was the matter? Who was this Mr. Gent, anyway? One of the FBI's Ten Most Wanted? Did Mr. Hodges think she was an accomplice in some kind of fraud?

She sat forward, tense, the urge to escape roaring like a lion in her brain. She quickly rejected the notion. That friendly security man who had escorted her to the Dragan headquarters was no doubt one of many security men who would track her attempted escape on a zillion security cameras and nab her before she made it to the main floor.

She felt lightheaded and realized she was hyperventilating. "Breathe deeply, slowly, you ninny!" she muttered. "Don't lose your nerve!" Angry with herself for letting her imagination run amok, she sat back, tried to relax. "Be logical," she told herself in a low, even whisper. "You haven't done anything wrong."

"Mr. Dragan?"

Lassiter didn't look up from his paperwork to press the intercom button. "Yes, Cindy?"

"I have Jessica Lubeck on the line."

Lassiter paused in his calculations, frowning. Why did that name sound familiar? "Who?"

"She's Managing Editor of *The Urban Sophisticate* magazine. This is her second call today."

Lassiter remembered. "Right," he murmured, annoyed with himself. He'd put her off all week, but he knew she needed an answer by the end of the workday. Though Lassiter wasn't a man to waver when a decision needed to be made, this time he was torn. "I'll take the call," he said, laying aside his pen.

"Line two, sir."

He picked up the receiver. "Hello, Ms. Lubek."

"Mr. Dragan," came the woman's husky voice. She sounded to be about fifty. "I hope you've decided to let *The Urban Sophisticate* do that 'Home For The Holidays With Lassiter Dragan' article."

"I'm flattered by the interest," he said, honestly. He'd been weighing the pros and cons all week.

"That doesn't sound like a firm yes," Jessica Lubek said. "What can I say to convince you? Have I mentioned our 'Home For The Holidays' issue is always our bestseller for the year?"

"Yes, Ms. Lubek," he said. "I know it would give Dragan Ventures invaluable exposure."

"Worth millions in advertising dollars. We have an international readership, as I believe I've mentioned."

"True." He paused. He'd already explained to her that he hadn't granted any interviews for years. Since she had been patient and was being so persistent, he decided to explain. "You see, Ms. Lubek—"

"Call me Jessica," she interrupted.

"Thank you, Jessica. Let me repeat, your offer intrigues me. It's just that the last time I was featured in a magazine, the experience wasn't one hundred percent positive."

"Really?" She paused, and Lassiter suspected she was puffing on a cigarette, no doubt the reason for her low, raspy voice. "Would you mind my asking what the problem was that's made you so publicity-shy?"

He glanced toward the window wall in his corner office, staring out at the overcast afternoon. Snow fell thick and fast. Traffic would be a bear getting home. He checked his watch. Three o'clock. He wished it were five. Wished this decision were made, once and for all. "I suppose you deserve to know, since I've kept you dangling all week," he said. "You see, five years ago, *Midas Touch Monthly* did a story on me. Do you know it?"

"Certainly. I read their article on you. It was a good piece.

Midas is a fine business magazine. Forgive my boasting, but its circulation is much smaller than ours.''

Lassiter's chuckle was ironic. "Exactly. But even with its limited circulation, after that article came out, I found myself…'' He paused. There wasn't a graceful way to put it, so he decided just to say it. "Well, due to that article, I found myself the matrimonial objective of a rabid horde of silly women.'' He cringed, recalling the havoc that experience wreaked.

"Oh?'' Jessica Lubek said, and he could hear her blow out smoke again. "That's a shame, Mr. Dragan.'' He detected the smile in her voice. "It must be hell being rich and handsome.''

He was surprised by the woman's bluntness. "You're quite right to be sardonic. Wealth has many perks. As for handsome, it's in the eye of the beholder. Unfortunately as far as I could tell, these women didn't care if I looked like a stubby wombat.''

"A stubby wombat?'' Jessica Lubek cut in, still sounding like she was grinning. "As I said, I did read the article, and it included a picture of you. In all honesty, Mr. Dragan, you look about as much like a stubby wombat as a prize stallion looks like a jackass.''

Lassiter experienced unease spiced with displeasure at her continued amusement at his expense. He supposed it could sound comical to someone who'd never experienced it. "The fact is, they wanted to marry rich, come Hades or high water, wombat or jackass. They camped outside my privacy gate, shrieking at me, throwing themselves on my car whenever I came and went. One had herself mailed to me in a huge box.''

He was surprised at how troubling the recollection was, even five years later. He was a private person, and his privacy had been blown all to blazes. "The intrusiveness became a hindrance. Women invaded my office building. I could get nothing done for a month.'' He picked up his gold pen and began a restless tapping on his desktop. "That's why I've refused to be featured in articles ever since.''

She chuckled aloud. "I know a lot of men who would do anything to get that kind of attention. Including my husband.''

"They should be wary of what they wish for. Trust me, being harassed by scheming, greedy women is no picnic." He leaned back in his chair and closed his eyes, exhausted and ambivalent. It had been a long, hectic week, and this was not what he needed right now. "I have to admit," he went on, "the article did bring me some lucrative clients, practically doubling my business."

"So you have a dilemma." She no longer sounded amused.

"Yeah," he said.

"I wish I could reassure you that it won't happen again, but I can't." She exhaled a prolonged blast of cigarette smoke, so audible he could almost smell it. "Publicity is a double-edged sword."

He clamped his jaws, brooding over whether the offer was a business opportunity he couldn't afford to refuse, or if he was insane to consider it? Was the untold wealth the publicity would bring worth the inevitable upheaval it would cause his well-ordered, intensely private lifestyle?

To Lassiter, everything was business-related. "Home" to him meant an investment, a tool to promote his company and increase his prosperity.

When asked about his heritage, Lassiter often joked, "Daddy was in steel—spell it any way you want," meaning "steel" or "steal." Lassiter was a bottom-line man. With anything he took on, he expected a profit. And this article would garner him a huge one.

That was why his hesitation to accept the offer annoyed him. *It should be a no-brainer!* But he also knew everything and everyone had a price. What price was he willing to pay for millions in free publicity?

What he needed was some way to benefit from the article without the disruptive burden of brazen, money-grubbing females. If he could just come up with a way to accomplish that.

"I gather none of them snared you?"

The question caught him off guard. "Excuse me?"

"I mean, I gather you're not married," the editor said.

Lassiter winced at the thought. To him, women were like anything else—assets or liabilities. On the asset side he counted the luscious "arm candy" he dated. Female liabilities included the screaming swarms that had invaded his home and business. The "assets" enjoyed the benefits of his luxurious lifestyle, for their companionship. Because they benefited for what they offered him, he never felt guilt or obligation once a relationship had run its course. As for marriage, he had no interest in "family." He saw no profit in it.

"Did you hear me?" Jessica asked.

"Yes, I—"

The double doors to Lassiter's office burst open to display a red-faced Herman Hodges framed in the space. He looked troubled and nervous. "Gent," he called out in a wheezy exhale.

Lassiter covered the receiver's mouthpiece. "Herm, I'm on a call."

The newcomer's inhale sounded like the gasp of a drowning man. He wagged his hands in front of him, as if to say that couldn't be helped. This was too important. Lassiter noticed he held something white.

"There's a woman in my office who gave me this napkin," he said, extending the flimsy paper toward Lassiter. "She said a *Mr. Gent* told her to come see me about a loan for a doggie salon." With a big gulp of air, he tramped into the large office, halting before his boss's vintage rosewood desk.

He yanked a handkerchief out of his hip pocket and wiped his sweat-beaded head. "It was a shocker seeing what looks amazingly like your signature on this—this coffee shop napkin." His expression became dubious. "Gent, old man, are *you* her Mr. Gent?"

The napkin! Lassiter sat forward, experiencing a curious, tingling shock. So, the coffee shop manager had taken him up on his offer.

"I've never known you to mix…" Herm swallowed, his jowls quivering as he loudly cleared his throat. "Well, to mix—shall we say—pleasure with business. *Lord,* Gent. Her business requirements, not to mention her lack of experience and collateral, were so diametrically opposed to what we do here, I gave her my cold-shoulder spiel, almost booted her out

of my office without a fare-thee-well! If she's a—a lady friend
of yours, you should have let me know…''

Lassiter recalled the woman's face, those big, vulnerable
green eyes—how they'd glimmered with horror and remorse
after she'd spilled coffee on his coat. He still couldn't figure
out what had come over him, made him behave so unchar-
acteristically, suggesting she contact Herm about a loan.
Maybe it was the season. He didn't ordinarily succumb to
anything as sappy as ''The Holiday Spirit.'' But what else
could explain it?

Lassiter's petite, grandmotherly executive assistant signaled
for his attention from the double-doored entry. She looked
worried. He nodded to reassure her that Herm's interruption
was okay. ''Hold on a second, Herm.'' Removing his hand
covering the telephone's mouthpiece, he said, ''Jessica, let me
get back with you in, say…'' He checked his wristwatch,
''…thirty minutes? I'll have a definite answer for you then.''

''Well, certainly…'' She sounded hesitant, puzzled, ''…as
long as your answer is yes.''

''Thirty minutes.'' He hung up and motioned Herm forward. ''Let's see that thing.'' It wasn't as though he expected
the napkin to be a forgery, but Herm needed to calm down or
he'd have a stroke.

Herm handed over the napkin.

''Sit down. Relax.'' Lassiter motioned toward one of the
twin navy, leather chairs placed within easy conversational
distance on the other side of his desk. ''What did you do, run
up the stairs? You look like you're going to explode.''

Herm collapsed into the armchair. ''Sure, sure, me run up
two flights of stairs. That'll be the day.''

Lassiter glanced at the napkin, then laid it aside. ''I'm sorry
I didn't mention Miss August.'' Miss August. *Trisha August.*
Interesting that her name had stuck in his mind. He went on,
''When the Randall deal heated up, it needed all my attention.
To be honest, I wasn't sure she'd come.'' He rested his fore-
arms on his desk. ''And she's not a girlfriend. I met her a few
days ago at a coffee shop. Suggesting she come here was—a
whim.'' He shrugged off his impulsiveness. ''It's Christmas.''

"A whim?" Herm repeated, his look scrutinizing. "It's *Christmas?*" His thick, gray eyebrows came together in a suspicious frown.

Lassiter's shrug had been the only explanation he intended to offer. In truth, it was all he had. "For whatever reason, I gave her your name. I thought she'd feel most comfortable with you. This place can be intimidating, and I've seen you with your grandchildren. You're a regular puppy dog."

"Puppy dog!" Herm made a pained face. "*Lord,* Gent! I might as well have dipped her in a vat of dry ice, I was so cold. I wish I'd known. I thought she was one of the innumerable square pegs we have to fend off." He blew out a breath. "And it's Friday afternoon—I'm tired." He ran his hands over his scalp, looking miserable. "I feel like a jerk."

"You did your job. You didn't know I sent her," Lassiter said. "Look at it this way. She'll forgive you when she walks out with the money."

Herm seemed to think about that, then nodded, though his brow was still furrowed. He crossed his arms over his belly. "O-kay," he said slowly. "So, Father Christmas, why did you send the pretty blonde to me, an old married man?" He eyed his boss with wry speculation. "Or do you see our two bachelor vice presidents as competition?"

Lassiter ignored his associate's gibe. "She needs a loan, not a lover."

Herm's expression grew wistful. "I'm sure you're right. To look at her, she's got to have all the lovers she can use."

Lassiter only half heard the comment. The telephone caught his attention and his promise to call Jessica Lubek came back to him. He glanced at his wristwatch. Twenty minutes left.

Trisha August's face affixed firmly in his mind, Lassiter recalled a question Jessica asked him just before Herm's intrusion. That question must have been skulking around his subconscious, because it suddenly came into sharp focus, and a thought struck. "I wonder," he mused aloud.

"I don't think there's much doubt about it," Herm said.

Lassiter looked up. "About what?"

Herm eyed his boss, his expression shifting to one of puzzlement. "About Miss August *not* needing a lover. Isn't that what we're talking about?"

"Oh—right." Lassiter's thoughts raced. He recalled how attractive she was, even in that atrocious uniform, and that hat that looked like it might take flight any second. Her hair had been pulled back into a tight bun at her nape. Even so, she was striking. Her eyes were the color of priceless jade, her facial bones delicately carved. Her lips were full, pink and her pale, flawless skin fairly glowed with golden undertones. She had a dainty, upturned nose, with the hint of a bump on its bridge. A slight flaw that made her nose a little crooked.

Lassiter wasn't accustomed to seeing flaws on faces as lovely as hers. The women he dated corrected such imperfections, enhanced cheeks and chin, lips and breasts. Trisha's slightly misaligned nose told him a great deal about her, and he liked what it said.

He'd bet a thousand shares of Dragan Ventures preferred stock that she rarely wore makeup, and the rosy flush of her cheeks and mouth was as natural as her strawberry-blond hair and her quaintly distinctive nose. "But she does need a loan." He sat back, his focus going inward.

Maybe. Just maybe it would work.

"I wonder," he said, thinking out loud. "She said she'd do anything for that loan." He stared, lost in his own thoughts.

"I don't like the look on your face, Gent."

Lassiter blinked, coming back to the present. He eyed the VP, his decision made. "Escort Miss August to my office."

Herm jumped, startled by the vehemence of Lassiter's command. He sat forward. "I thought you were playing Father Christmas for this woman. What is this dark—*thing* I see in your eyes?" He glowered, his lips working, as though he were having trouble voicing his misgivings. "You wouldn't—it would be unethical to—to—" He hefted himself out of the chair. "What are you *thinking?* Didn't you say, yourself, she doesn't need a lover?"

Unaccustomed to being challenged by employees, no matter how well-meaning, Lassiter couldn't mask his impatience. "Neither do *I*," he growled.

CHAPTER THREE

TRISHA found herself being guided out of Herman Hodges' office through the plush reception area of Dragan Ventures. Wearing shoes on the cushy, beige carpeting seemed like a sin.

Mr. Hodges carried her folder and had draped her overcoat across one arm. He held her elbow in a gentlemanly way, his attitude much warmer and friendlier than when he'd rushed out of his office twenty minutes ago. He lead her into the entry hall, with walls and floors of polished green marble, to a bank of elevators in an alcove. A window wall exhibited a snow-covered panorama of downtown Kansas City, glass and steel skyscrapers, blurred behind an undulating veil of white.

"It looks like the snow is letting up," Mr. Hodges said, drawing her from her nervous thoughts.

"Yes," she said, not knowing quite how to react to the man's one hundred and eighty degree reversal in attitude. He was smiling so she smiled back, though her effort was half-hearted. "Um—Mr. Hodges," she asked. "Where did you say we were going?" She wanted to make absolutely sure she hadn't misunderstood when he'd told her before. The shock had been so great, she hadn't been able to ask him to repeat himself until this minute.

He pressed the elevator "up" button. "To Mr. Dragan's office."

She heard him say the same words he'd said before, but they still didn't make sense. Why would he take her to Mr. Dragan's office? "Oh?" He seemed too friendly to be about to accuse her of anything. Still, she worried about Mr. Gent. She hadn't imagined Herman Hodges' distress at the mention of his name. He'd been frantic. What had happened in the past twenty minutes to change his attitude? "May I ask why we're going there?"

The elevator door opened and Mr. Hodges urged her inside a mirrored enclosure. She couldn't miss the fleeting frown that crossed his face. He obviously wasn't happy about his errand.

Oh dear, she cried inwardly, *it has something to do with Mr. Gent! She felt it all the way to her toes! That darn napkin! If I hadn't dragged that out, I'd be on the bus by now, safely out of the Dragan building on my way home.*

"Mr. Dragan wants to—speak with you," Herman Hodges said. Trisha watched his face in the mirrored interior. He looked a little guilty, reluctant, like a man leading a lamb to slaughter.

"I see." She clenched the thin shoulder strap of her handbag. She didn't really see at all. Once again, the idea of running crossed her mind. But that would be cowardly. Besides, how many times did she have to remind herself that she'd done absolutely nothing wrong?

She shifted her gaze to the flash of the floor indicator. The indicator flashed "fifty-one," then "fifty-two," where it stopped. The ride had been short. Too short. When the door whooshed open, Mr. Hodges guided Trisha out into a dramatic marble foyer with a twenty-foot ceiling. Across from the elevator alcove a pair of huge copper doors stood open, revealing a large room beyond. Was it Mr. Dragan's office? The lump of fear in Trisha's throat prevented her from asking.

Mr. Hodges took her arm, guiding her through the double doors. The room they entered had very high ceilings. The furnishings were elegant, understated, a mix of leathers, silks and tapestries. Live plants abounded in huge planters, many the size of trees.

"It's—it's quite beautiful." Glancing around Trisha noticed both sides of the huge room were entirely glass. Even on a sullen, overcast day like today, natural light flooded the place.

"Yes, it is nice." Mr. Hodges kept his focus straight ahead, toward the far end of the room where another set of tall, copper doors loomed. Dread at what waited behind those doors made her heart pound and her stomach churn. Why did Mr.

Dragan want to speak *personally* with her? This fifty-second floor was definitely the inner sanctum of Dragan Ventures. A person either had to be very fortunate to get in here—or in a *lot* of trouble.

"What—what is a room like this used for?" she asked, needing to get her mind on something besides her immediate future. If she didn't she was afraid her heart might explode from the stress.

"It's our executive lounge."

"I gather your executives don't lounge much," she said, noting the room was empty.

"It's Christmas. Many of our employees take vacations at this time of year."

They reached the double doors and Mr. Hodges opened one. Beyond was a room that finally looked like an office, a cheery one, ornamented with artistic arrangements of lively watercolors. Once again, both side walls were entirely glass.

In front of each window wall was a desk, at each desk a woman sat, working at her computer. As Mr. Hodges and Trisha entered, the two female employees glanced up and smiled. The fact that they hadn't stared daggers at her wasn't much of a relief, since it was unlikely they would be privy to why she was there. She wondered if they would look at her differently when she left.

The next set of double doors opened on a pleasant, carpeted room, its walls papered with a subtle, textured design and arranged with impressionistic pen-and-ink drawings. Slightly left of center, facing them, a woman about Herman Hodges' age sat behind a desk. Petite, with neatly permed white hair, the attractive woman glanced up from her computer screen and smiled.

"Cindy, this is Miss August."

"Of course." The woman pressed a button, announcing Trisha's arrival.

A man responded with, "Send her in." The voice was deep and deadly serious. Had she come to the end of her journey? Did she at last stand at the mouth of the dragon's lair—the penthouse office of the legendary Lassiter Q. Dragan?

The air suddenly seemed frigid. Trisha felt chilled through, and weak in the knees. She squeezed Mr. Hodges' arm tighter in an effort to remain upright.

He must have noticed, for he glanced at her. "Are you all right?"

She wasn't, but she didn't intend to turn into a Weeping Wanda. She and her mom had weathered many storms, just the two of them. If there was one thing Trisha had learned from her mother, it was to face life with a positive attitude. Concentrating on her mother's good advice, Trisha managed a confident expression. "I'm fine."

He patted her hand, resting on his arm. "I'll leave you now." He walked her to the door and grasped the handle, then hesitated. Leaning close, he murmured, "Do what you feel in your heart is best—for you." His features were troubled.

She stared, unsure how to react. *Do what you feel in your heart is best—for you!* Was it advice or a warning?

With a nod of encouragement, he handed her her file folder and coat and opened the door, moving away as he did.

Lost in her mental quandary, she belatedly responded with a half nod, which probably looked more like a convulsive tic than a reply.

"Come in, Miss August."

The booming command from beyond the door made her jump. On their own, her legs moved forward. It wasn't until after she felt a puff of air at her back, and heard the door whisper shut, that she managed to focus on the man across the room. He sat behind a large desk, the wall beyond him solid glass.

He rose to stand. Silhouetted against the window, he was little more than a black shape, a tall, broad-shouldered shadow-man. Since he wore no suit coat, his dress shirt was the most visible thing about him. The expanse of whiteness was bisected down the center by a dark tie.

He motioned her forward. "Please, come. Sit down."

Though his invitation into the room had been forceful, his tone was less formidable now, more inviting.

"Yes, sir." She walked toward the proffered chair. By the

time she came within reach of his desk, her eyes had adjusted, and she could see his face. Shock made her stumble to a halt. "Oh...it's—it's..." She couldn't believe her eyes. The man from the coffee shop! The man she'd drenched with Colombian Dark Secret! "Mr. *Gent?*" She didn't know what to think. "I—I thought I was here to see Mr. Dragan."

He motioned her toward the chair. "Please sit down, Miss August. I'll explain."

She canted her head in the direction of the chair, but had a hard time removing her gaze from his face. Finally, she shifted her attention to the armchair, sidled to it and sat down. But if he thought sitting would mean relaxing, he vastly misjudged her mental state. She sat erect, clutching her coat and her folder to her. "I'm sitting." Her tone held a surprising edge, considering how nervous she was. But she wanted answers.

He remained standing. "Would you care for coffee?"

She shook her head. "I get plenty of coffee, thanks."

He grasped the irony and pursed his lips. "Right." He surprised her by circling his desk and standing before her. She caught a whiff of his aftershave, tangy and masculine, like a cool breeze through a pine forest with the hint of smoke from a distant campfire. "May I have your coat, Miss August? I'll hang it up for you."

She'd forgotten she had it and looked down, noticing she was crushing it to her, along with her poor folder. Annoyed with herself for showing anxiety in her body language, she tried to relax. "Why—yes, thanks." Their eyes met in a brief, electric shock. During the three days since she'd seen him, her imaginings had degraded badly. Those eyes, the color of polished steel, were so striking that to look at them made breathing difficult. She handed him her coat, then busied herself smoothing her crinkled folder on her lap.

"You're welcome," he said, but she avoided glancing his way. Flattening her hands on the folder, she stared out the window behind his desk. She could hear him move across the carpet as he deposited her coat somewhere. She continued to watch the snow flutter down. She breathed deeply, working on her poise.

After a moment he crossed her line of vision. Even the fleeting shadow moving before her made her pulse jump. So much for the calming influence of fluttering snow!

She found herself once again staring at the man as he took a seat and folded his hands on his desktop. She looked at his fingernails. They didn't shine with polish, but they were neatly trimmed. His fingers were long and graceful, in the most masculine sense of the word. Her gaze trailed over his torso, taking in broad shoulders, strong arms, muscular chest and taut belly. Those attributes not only refused to be camouflaged by his crisp, white shirt, but were somehow magnified. It almost seemed as though nature had taken special pains forming and perfecting him and then made sure no mere piece of cloth could mask such exquisite handiwork.

"Miss August, I'm sorry for the confusion," he said, drawing her gaze to his sharp, arresting features. "My name is Dragan, Lassiter Dragan. However, some of my business associates know me as Gent." He paused, looking at her with such intensity she felt it physically, a low humming in the center of her chest. It didn't help ease her breathing. "You see, Gent is a nickname."

She found herself biting her lower lip and made herself stop. That would be a clear sign of distress. "Oh?" she said "Then—why?" was all she could say.

"Why didn't I tell you who I am?"

She nodded. Was the man clairvoyant? The notion that such a handsome man could read her mind was disconcerting. On the other hand, if he could not only ask the questions, but answer them, too, it would make her malfunctioning mental processes less of a stumbling block.

"I'm a private person, Miss August," he began. "It's no secret that my name is well known in Kansas City. I was in a hurry that day, and signing Gent saved time." He glanced at his wristwatch, then back at her, as though the mention of time reminded him he was on a tight schedule. She wondered how many minutes he'd allotted for her. Peeking at her own watch, she noticed it was three-twenty-five. "I didn't anticipate meeting with you myself,'' he said. ''I don't often handle preliminary meetings.''

She was confused. ''So—why am I here?''

He smiled briefly, the glint of his teeth disarming, yet strangely ominous. She experienced a skittering along her spine and couldn't be sure what it meant—attraction? Foreboding? She had a feeling it was a little of both. ''I'm glad you're a woman who likes to get to the point.'' His gaze was steady, steely. ''It's important that we do.''

''Please—go on,'' she said. Her pounding heart couldn't stand much more punishment. Was it possible he *might* be considering giving her a loan? She threw out a silent prayer.

''The reason I had you see Herman Hodges was because I felt you needed a break. I get feelings about people, Miss August, and I felt you might be a good risk,'' he said. ''My initial thought was to loan you the twenty-five thousand you want.''

Her heart soared. She smiled and opened her mouth to begin an effusive thank you, along with a thousand reassurances that he wouldn't be sorry for putting his faith in her. But before she could speak, he held up a halting hand.

''However, something's come up that has made me rethink my original idea. Something that I feel could benefit us both.'' He paused, his nostrils flared, and his jaw muscles flexed. It seemed as though he was having trouble stating his proposal.

''Tell me, Mr. Dragan.'' She was almost sick with excitement. She'd come here expecting accusations, a reprimand at the least. Now, suddenly, a rich and powerful venture capitalist was actually talking about loaning her money. It didn't seem possible. But she wasn't dreaming. She bit the inside of her cheek and it hurt, so she knew she was really here. ''I—I can make a success of Dog Days of August. All I need is the chance.''

''I'm sure that's true.'' He relaxed back in his big, executive chair. ''That's why I'm prepared to offer you not only the bare-bones twenty-five thousand you need, but an additional twenty-five thousand, to upgrade the operation—and at the prime interest rate.''

Trisha sat stunned. She wanted to scream with joy, but a tiny fragment of her mind sensed his offer was a smoke screen to obscure some hidden agenda. She didn't want to believe that, but no matter how she tried to shake off the feeling, it nagged. "I—I'm…" She swallowed to steady her voice. "I'm flattered, Mr. Dragan," she said. "But, why? Why would you do such a generous thing for me, when nobody else would give me the time of day?"

She recalled Mr. Hodges' initial reaction to her business plan, and cruel doubt clutched at her heart. "Just now, downstairs, I was being rushed out the door until Mr. Hodges saw that napkin. And you haven't even looked at my business plan." She frowned, her initial excitement fading fast. "I hate to slit my own throat, but considering you're supposed to be a shrewd money man, this doesn't seem like a smart way to do business."

"The situation is unusual, Miss August." His lips curved in a half smile that made her heart flutter and her nerves buzz ominously. "I have a small problem." He paused for a moment. The silence in the room was heavy, almost too much for Trisha's strained nerves to endure. "It's very simple," he said. "You help me and I'll help you."

"Help you how?" She feared whatever he asked her to do—for fifty-thousand dollars—wouldn't be easy. But hadn't she sworn she would do anything for a loan? Hadn't she sworn it out loud? And within earshot of this very man? She felt her face heat. What on earth was he thinking? "I won't do anything illegal!"

"I wouldn't ask you to, Miss August," he said. "It's perfectly legitimate. All I need from you is a little 'sweat equity,' beginning this weekend and ending New Year's Day."

The words "sweat equity" stuck in her mind. What did he mean by "sweat equity?" The only picture that flared in her mind was obscenely risqué—silk sheets, naked bodies, limbs entwined in passion.

Mr. Hodges' warning came back to her and she felt mortified. Had he known Mr. Dragan's intentions? With a half groan, half growl, she vaulted up. "I've never been so insulted! Offering me money for—for…'' She couldn't bring herself to say it. "Maybe I didn't make myself clear, Mr. Dragan.'' Her tone was as irate as her glare. "I won't do anything illegal or—or…'' She rang her hands, hesitating. "I was going to say *immoral*. I know in this day and age that sounds outdated, but—''

"Yes, it does,'' he said, then pursed his lips suspiciously. Was he laughing at her?

"So, you admit it!'' she cried. Moving away from her chair, she took a step backward, bent on a swift escape.

"Miss August.'' He rose to his feet, as though he might attempt to physically bar her exit. "You misunderstand. I don't intend to lay a hand on you.''

She had whirled away and taken several steps toward the exit, but his response made her stop and peer at him over her shoulder. "No?''

He leaned forward, resting his hands on his desk. "No.'' He shook his head.

She saw the truth in his serious features and turned around, wayward curiosity and her desperation for a loan getting the better of her. "Then what sort of—sweat equity are you talking about that would make you require my—er—*me*—over the holidays?''

"I need a wife.''

Her jaw dropped. She'd half expected him to say he needed someone to paint the entire outside of the Dragan building, or to leap out of an airplane with an experimental parachute made of pasta. Something dangerous and foolhardy. But she never expected him to suggest anything as dangerous and foolhardy as, *"I need a wife!''* Her alarmed expression must have been hilarious, because he flashed that troubling, sardonic grin. "I repeat, Miss August. Not *that* kind of sweat equity. Your quaint notion of immorality aside, paying a woman for sex falls under the heading of 'illegal.' Our relationship would be entirely legal, and purely business.''

She stared, tongue-tied.

Apparently laboring under the delusion that she had any intention of agreeing, he went on, "You would receive an appropriate wardrobe, spend a luxurious vacation at my estate, pretending to be my bride for a magazine article. Then, after the new year, you collect fifty-thousand dollars. At prime.'' He paused, watching her. When she didn't respond, he straightened and crossed his arms over his chest. "*Nobody* loans money at the prime rate, Miss August. Only Santa Claus, himself, might make you a better offer, but I wouldn't hold my breath.'' With the ill-omened lift of an eyebrow, he added, "You would be insane to say no.''

Her incredulity at his arrogance and audacity surged and overflowed. "Then I'm definitely insane.'' She straightened her shoulders. "And proud to be!'' Out of the corner of her eye she noticed pages from her folder scattered over the floor, and had a split-second urge to stoop down and gather them. But almost immediately she decided against it. If there had ever been a time she needed to march regally away from any man and any proposition, this was that time! With a stiff arm, she indicated her spilled business plan. "Have your secretary mail my prospectus to me, Mr. Dragan! *Goodbye!*''

"I hope, in ten years, when you're still serving coffee, you don't look back and regret this decision.''

She already regretted it, recalling her frantic vow. *"I'll do anything to get this loan! Anything!"* Halfway to the door, she found her firm resolve faltering. She slowed, then stopped. A voice in her head shouted, *"What's so offensive about pretending to be a gorgeous, wealthy man's wife? Not to mention getting a free wardrobe of beautiful clothes and a vacation at a palatial estate—and finally, fifty-thousand dollars to finance your dream! If you say no to this you really are insane!"*

Reluctantly, half ashamed of herself for caving in, she faced him. Her cheeks burned, so she must be blushing furiously. To salve her pride, she set her features defiantly. "Absolutely no hanky-panky!''

He shook his head. "I promise.''

"But why me? Surely you have girlfriends who'd do you this favor—and without the no-hanky-panky rule.''

"I prefer to keep relationships on a *quid pro quo* basis.''

He indicated her with a casual wave. "You want something from me and I want something from you. *Quid pro quo.*"

She scoffed, "That's very romantic."

He eyed her levelly. "I don't mean it to be, Miss August."

He certainly sounded like he meant what he said. But she'd met a lot of men who'd said things they didn't mean, made promises they broke with shameful ease. Lassiter Dragan was an extraordinarily sexy man, with bedroom eyes that seduced without even trying. Would this favor he was asking truly be all business? Did she really want it to be? When he didn't need her any longer, would she be proud of herself or would she feel cheap and weak and used? Even with this cautionary thought skulking around in her brain, she couldn't quite convince herself to walk away. There was something in his eyes that held her. "What did you say you needed a wife for?" she asked, struggling to find something, anything, to help her make a logical, intelligent decision.

"A magazine wants to interview me." Rounding his desk he walked all the way across his office to the opposite wall, paneled in cherry wood. "Being interviewed for a magazine has caused me trouble in the past—with women." His tone and his profile made his annoyance clear.

"Women?" she echoed. That was an odd reason to... "Oh?" Maybe that was why he'd promised he wouldn't lay a hand on her!

He had touched a panel and it opened to reveal a closet. In the act of reaching for her coat, he shifted his gaze her way. Those sexy, languid eyelids narrowed significantly. "No, Miss August. Not *'oh?'*"

She shook her head, her eyebrows going up in question. "Not—oh?"

"Absolutely. *Not!*" He made the assertion slowly and precisely, his features stony. "After the last magazine article, women came out of the woodwork. They surrounded my home. Camped out at my gate. Threw themselves onto my car. Invaded my office. Silly, shallow, avaricious woman who just wanted to marry rich. I don't care to go through that again.

That's what I meant when I said women had caused me trouble.'' His lips dipped in a deeper frown. ''Is that clear?''

The picture he painted seemed quite possible, considering how handsome he was, and how wealthy. She nodded. ''Crystal.''

''Then you understand why appearing to have a wife would simplify things for me.''

''Yes, I see.'' For once today, she finally did see.

''And you don't find it funny?'' he asked.

She shrugged. ''I can see how it wouldn't be.''

For a long moment he watched her, his severe expression unnerving. ''Thank you,'' he said, at last.

''For what?''

''For not finding it funny.'' He shifted his attention to the closet and drew out her coat. Draping it over an arm he walked to her with it. ''This article is a good business opportunity for me. Because it is, and because of my past negative experience, it could be a good business opportunity for you, too.'' He held up her coat so that she could slip her arms in it. As she did, he murmured into her hair, ''So you accept my deal?''

The feel of his warm breath at her nape made her tingle and she shivered with its effect. Pulling her coat around her, she faced him.

For a moment she looked inward, weighing the pros and cons. Did she dare turn down a loan at prime? Over the life of the loan, she'd save well over five-thousand dollars. But pretending to be his wife? Was this right? Was it wrong? Would she regret it if she said no? If she said yes? Was she as serious about wanting to start her own business as she'd told herself she was?

She had a thought and had to ask. ''But what about when the article comes out? People will think we're married.''

He made a dismissive gesture. ''It's *The Urban Sophisticate*'s 'Christmas In July' issue. That's over a half year away. Plenty of marriages break up before six months. You can tell anyone who asks that we were rash, and it's over.'' His deep-timbered voice was so pleasant to listen to, she found herself hanging on every word. He could have been reciting the coffee shop menu and it would have sounded like poetry spoken in his low, seductive way. "As far as the article goes, together you and I can only do ourselves good—for both our businesses."

Trisha absorbed his comment. His proposition was outlandish to say the least. But if he felt strongly enough about needing a wife to ask her to help him, then in his opinion she had worth and value. He'd proved that with his fifty-thousand dollar loan offer. Amazing! A wealthy, powerful man wanted *her* help and was willing to pay very well for it.

She felt strangely empowered. It was a nice feeling, one she'd rarely experienced. Certainly her boss, Ed, had never made her feel worthy of her seven-dollars-an-hour salary.

And besides making her feel better about herself, in less than two weeks, Mr. Dragan would loan her the money to make her dream a reality. How close to a miracle did she need to get before she was willing to reach out and grab it?

Yes, she deserved this chance. What did it matter if it came with a few odd strings attached? Why shouldn't she accept his proposition? Deciding she'd be crazy not to, she stretched out a hand. "*I do,* Mr. Dragan," she said, deliberately mimicking the marriage ceremony's solemn vow. Any wedding—even a sham wedding—between millionaire venture capitalist Lassiter Q. Dragan and wannabe-doggie-salon-owner Trisha Marie August, demanded a touch of irony.

He took her hand in his, warm, firm and flustering. The wry quirk of his lips told her he detected her mockery. "You've made a wise decision," he said. "I'll have my chauffeur meet you in the executive lounge. He'll take you home to pack."

"Pack?" she asked, too aware that he still held her hand.

"Yes, Miss August," He released her fingers only to skim his hand along her arm to her elbow. His trailing fingers made her tingle, though he touched nothing more intimate than her coat sleeve. "We're flying to Las Vegas tonight."

"We are?"

"For the ruse." He glanced her way. "Being the quickie marriage capital of the world, spending the weekend there will make an impetuous wedding between us seem more believable.''

''Oh…'' She nodded. It made sense.

''You'll want to buy clothes while we're there,'' he added, guiding her toward the exit.

''Oh—yes…'' They hadn't left his office yet, and her head was already spinning, while he seemed to have everything worked out. She experienced a flash of misgiving as reality started to settle in. ''Uh—Mr. Dragan, I'm not quite sure—''

''My chauffeur will drive you to the Dragan hangar at the airport,'' he said, cutting her off. She sensed the interruption had been calculated to block her ability to express any qualms. ''I'll meet you by my plane by seven.''

He opened the office door for her, his manner gallant, but preemptory, making it clear that the subject was closed. The die cast. Their handshake binding. ''Now if you'll excuse me?'' His lips curved in a polite, half smile that didn't register in his eyes. ''I need to make a phone call.''

CHAPTER FOUR

LASSITER arrived at the Dragan hangar precisely at seven o'clock. Bypassing the covered parking slots at the front of the building, he drove through a ten-foot, chain-link gate, across the snow-cleared tarmac, pulling into the cavernous hangar. His company jet sat outside, ready to taxi to the runway. One of his two pilots, clad in a crisp, black uniform and black-and-gold billed cap, held Miss August's bag as he aided her up the fold-out steps.

Lassiter's female passenger wore the same knee-length, black coat and black pumps she'd worn when she left his office. Her handbag swung from a long, thin strap over her shoulder. She wore no hat. Her arms were bent, as though she held something, but he couldn't see what it was.

Since the sun had set hours ago, the hangar lights were the only illumination. Being high wattage spots, they made her blond hair easy to see. Just past shoulder-length, not too curly and not too straight, it fluttered in the wintry gusts.

Lassiter pulled his suitcase from the passenger seat of his sports car, his gaze remaining on her as she disappeared into the sleek, silver and sky-blue jet. "You should wear your hair down all the time," he murmured with a reflective half smile, recalling his first glimpse of her that afternoon.

He'd known she was attractive, even wearing that atrocious uniform and bat-wing hat, her hair skinned back in a bun. But when she'd walked into his office, he'd been blown away. The copper doors were the consummate backdrop, a perfect contrast for her trim, emerald blazer and slender, matching skirt.

She'd been breathtaking, a work of art, her clothes bringing out the jewel-green color of her huge, anxious eyes. Even her snowy blouse gave him pause, the way its ruffled collar accentuated her slender, oh so delectable neck. Though the combination of tasteful ruffles and pale skin was cunning in its artistry, Lassiter sensed she had not planned it.

Her hair, free flowing as it was now, had dramatized and underscored the grace and elegance of her bone structure, like a golden frame around a warm and luminous Renoir. Seeing her standing there had been such unadulterated drama, he'd experienced an odd, prickling shock, and almost found himself letting out a low wolf whistle of surprise. He'd stopped himself just in time. What a daft reaction to the mere appearance of a woman. It wasn't as though he was unaccustomed to beautiful women. Even so, he'd had the most peculiar urge to grab his suit jacket, suddenly regretting meeting her in his shirtsleeves.

That, too, had been an absurd impulse. After all, he'd been about to make her an offer she couldn't refuse. There had been no need to impress her. Even so, for some bizarre reason, he'd opted to wear a suit to Las Vegas tonight, rather than jeans and a turtleneck sweater. He still had trouble figuring out that decision. This was a vacation weekend, not a starched corporate jaunt where he had to play CEO.

"Sir, may I take your bag?"

Lassiter blinked, realizing his chief pilot had approached him . "Thank you, Kent." He handed over his suitcase. "I gather Miss August is settled in?"

"Yes, sir."

They walked toward the plane. A few flakes of snow cavorted in the spotlights' glow. "What does the weather look like?"

"We have a few low clouds, but we'll be above the weather shortly after takeoff, so I anticipate a smooth flight."

"Good."

When they reached the jet, the pilot stepped back to allow Lassiter to climb the four steps into the forward section of the passenger area. He entered just behind a mahogany-paneled bulkhead, the food and drink compartments separating the cockpit from the remainder of the plane.

Since the only other person in the passenger section was Trisha August, Lassiter found her immediately. She no longer wore her coat. Apparently the copilot had taken it upon himself to hang it in the rear closet. And why not? He was a young, attractive man and Miss August was also young and attractive. Though the aviator would know better than to trifle with a woman who, for whatever reason, was a guest of Lassiter's, he would be anxious to please.

Trisha sat in one of the white, leather bucket seats three-quarters of the way back in the twelve passenger jet, the fifth of six seats on the opposite side of the cabin. Lassiter found that amusing. It was as though she assumed she must sit in "coach."

"Miss August," he said, straightening after ducking through the entryway. "You needn't sit back there. All the seats cost the same."

She looked up, seeming startled to see him, which was a ridiculous assumption for him to jump to. She knew he would be there. Perhaps she was nervous. That would be understandable. Many people had a fear of flying. He approached her along the narrow aisle between leather seats, elevated on a platform a foot above the walkway. "If you're afraid to fly, don't worry. My pilots are very conservative. When the weather isn't optimal, they won't fly."

She smiled, a charming sight. "Oh—I'm not afraid." It was at that moment Lassiter noticed a white, furry creature, curled in her lap. "I was talking to Perrier. She's a little fidgety. She's never been on an airplane."

Lassiter had difficulty believing his eyes. "You brought a *dog?*" It came out sounding more like an accusation than he intended.

She stroked the animal's back. Her smile disappeared, disquiet taking its place. "Yes. I—I hope you don't mind, but…" She cuddled it to her breast as though fearing he might wrench it from her hands and toss it into a snowbank. "I rescued her from the side of a road when she was a puppy. We've never been separated overnight. She's only eight pounds and very well-behaved. She won't be any bother."

Lassiter experienced a surge of aggravation. He'd never been able to understand the strange attachment people had for their pets. It seemed foolishly sentimental to lavish devotion on a dumb animal, but if she had to have the beast, it made little difference to their plan. Eyeing the dog severely, he had a thought. A dog could add a homey touch for the magazine article.

His annoyance ebbed. Now that he saw her pet as an asset, he wanted to ease her concern, and leaned forward to stroke the small, kinky-curly head. "Had you asked to bring the dog, my first reaction would have been negative, but I've decided it can be an advantage. Lots of people like dogs. Odds are, some animal lovers out there could be so taken with your mutt, they'll decide to come to me with business ventures."

Trisha didn't speak for a moment, her expression going skeptical. "Oh?" she finally said. "Well, I'm gratified my dog *works* for you." Her tone was hard-edged. "Maybe we should rent a couple of children. I've heard people like *them,* too."

He straightened, taken aback by her sarcasm. "I think a dog is enough."

He wasn't accustomed to nervy retorts, especially from subordinates. Of course, this was an unusual case. She wasn't an employee. For the next ten days, Trisha August would play his *wife*. Rather than find her insubordination annoying, he found it oddly stimulating. He only hoped he didn't find her *too* stimulating. He'd made her a promise about that.

"What did you do about your job?"

She remained sober. "Ed knew I was applying for a loan to start my own business, so he knew I might be leaving at a moment's notice. His nephew needed a job, so it's taken care of."

"Convenient the nephew needed work."

She shrugged. "I hope he'll work out. He needs a job almost monthly."

Lassiter found her remark amusing but she wasn't smiling so he didn't. He indicated the forward portion of the seating area. "Wouldn't you rather move up to the front?"

"No, thank you. I'm fine." Trisha turned to stare out the window. She couldn't have made it any clearer that she was annoyed. *Why in Hades was she annoyed?* Hadn't he reassured her that her blasted dog was welcome?

He scanned her profile, tense and fixed. "If you're hungry, there's iced shrimp cocktail and—"

"I ate a peanut butter sandwich before I left." She glanced at him, her chin high. "Thank you, anyway." Averting her gaze, she went back to staring into the night.

She might be offended, but at least she was being civil. That's all he really asked of her—until the *Urban Sophisticate*'s cameras began clicking away. "All right, then." He decided standing there pondering her temperament was counterproductive. "I have work to do, so I'll leave you to your—thoughts." *Whatever the blazes they are!*

He indicated the area beneath her window. "There's a tabletop in that slot. If you decide you want anything to eat just lift it out. Usually I have a hostess do the serving, but one's on vacation and the other is down with the flu, so feel free to scavenge through the food and beverage compartments. There are snacks, whole meals, desserts, drinks and a microwave oven if you want anything heated." He started to turn away, then shifted back. "Oh, if you need more leg room, the chairs swivel toward the center of the cabin." He indicated the lever. "Once we take off, make yourself comfortable."

"Mr. Dragan?"

At the sound of his chief pilot's voice, Lassiter turned toward the front. The trim, compact, man of forty had closed the exit door and stood before the paneled bulkhead. "We'll be taxiing to the runway in a moment."

"Thanks, Kent."

The pilot disappeared behind the bulkhead, joining the co-pilot in the cockpit.

Returning his attention to Trisha, Lassiter said, "If you'll excuse me?"

Pretty and peeved and gravely dignified, she nodded, continuing to stare out of her window.

The plane took off and Trisha stared, unseeing, at the blackness of night, thirty-thousand feet above earth. She could hardly fathom how her life had changed so much in one single day. Here she was, in the middle of a high-priced and well-paying ruse, flying to Las Vegas in Lassiter Dragan's private jet, simply to validate a story of a quickie marriage.

Every time she thought about what she'd agreed to do, she had to fight off nagging doubts about her sanity. Then she would remind herself of the fifty-thousand dollars, and realize she was not only sane but one of the luckiest people in the world.

She looked at Perrier, snoozing in her lap. After the first G-force panic of takeoff, the dog had settled down and was blissfully asleep. Trisha glanced up to focus on the back of Mr. Dragan's head. He had such neatly trimmed hair, so dark, yet glistening with highlights. If she were a betting woman, she'd wager it was soft, and smelled good, too.

She flinched at the waywardness of her thought. She was still put out with him, and a little disappointed. He *hated* animals. Well, that might be too strong a word. But he was no fan. For a brief, painful moment, he'd reminded her of her father. She didn't like the comparison to a man who'd been so wrapped up in "growing the business" as he'd put it, that he never had time for his wife and daughter—let alone animals.

For as far back as Trisha could remember, she'd taken in strays. She'd lugged in cats almost as big as she was. Some of the dogs had been bigger. Her father never failed to rant and rave, shouting that they were unsanitary, disease carrying, smelly, money-wasting pains, and he wouldn't allow the mangy things to stay. Luckily for both Trisha and the animals she brought home, her father spent little time away from his office. He never entered her room. So she managed to keep a needy, stray dog or cat hidden from him until she could find it a home.

When her dad finally left for good, Trisha had been eight. At long last, she was able to have pets of her own, though she and her mother had moved into a little apartment hardly big enough for the two of them. Even so, Trisha and her mother found great joy in their rescued dogs and cats. Trisha felt in her heart that she and her mom were happier in their cut-rate, two room apartment with grateful, loving animals, than her dad was in his ritzy condo, no matter how much he relished "growing the business." Eventually her father had become a wealthy man, a so-called pillar of Kansas City society. He was up to his third—or was it his fourth wife?

Trisha hadn't seen him from the day he walked out, and she never wanted to see him, ever again. While away from the house, *growing his business,* he'd neglected his wife, Maggie, and his little daughter. When he was home, he'd bullied them so unmercifully that after the divorce Maggie refused child support. She even refused to keep his name, changing both hers and Trisha's back to her maiden name, August.

Trisha's mother had also demanded "no contact" between Trisha and her father. Though they both knew he would oppose being forced to give financial support, and would never visit his daughter, the idea that he might have, given the chance, was a lie they told each other. Neither wanted to think of him as the utterly callous man he was.

The way her father felt about animals, and the way Lassiter Dragan had glowered at Perrier, brought bad memories rushing back. It had made her think, at least for the moment, that Lassiter and her father were alike. Since she had agreed to spend the Christmas holidays with Mr. Dragan, she'd been momentarily unsettled, even angry, at the need to spend time around *any* man who was *anything* like her father.

Now that she'd had some time to think about it, she was ashamed of herself for her knee-jerk reaction. She'd been snappish with her host. An apology was in order. After all, Lassiter Dragan was the only person, out of the dozens she'd asked, offering her a chance to go after her dream. She owed him for that! It was a shame if he wasn't an animal person, but that was none of her business.

She looked down at Perrier, sleeping peacefully. "Sorry, sweetie." She lifted the dog as she stood. "I have to speak with Mr. Dragan." She settled her pet in the chair. Perrier blinked and sat up. "You sleep." Trisha patted the dog's head. "I'll be back in a few minutes."

Perrier seemed to understand. She lay her head on her front paws and closed her eyes.

Gingerly, so as not to make loud, jarring noises, Trisha held on to the chair in front of her to make the long step down to the walkway. Nervous, she made her way to the front seat where Mr. Dragan sat, the polished wood tabletop pulled out, his laptop opened. He appeared to be reading something on the Internet.

Ashamed and tongue-tied, she leaned on the chair opposite Mr. Dragan to put as much distance between them as possible. It wasn't much, since the aisle was a scant two feet wide. When he didn't seem to notice that she'd joined him, she cleared her throat.

He turned, his expression shifting from concentration to curiosity. "Is there something I can do for you?"

She nodded, taking a deep breath. "Yes, you can accept my apology." She waved toward the back, where she'd been sitting. "I was rude."

She watched as his only reaction was the slight lift of one eyebrow. "You were?"

She clasped her hands before her. "You don't have to pretend you didn't notice. It's very gentlemanly, but..." She paused, a thought striking. "Is that why your nickname's Gent? Because you're a gentleman?"

His lips quirked in a wry grin. "A reporter from the *Wall Street Journal* once referred to me in an article as 'The Gentleman Dragon.' He seemed to fall into deep reflection for a few seconds, looking past her. She could tell when he came back, because his gaze returned to hers. "I don't recall his reason, but since then, close friends in the business have called me Gent." He closed his laptop. "I've never thrown a cloak over a mud puddle for a lady to walk across, so don't take it too much to heart."

She shook her head at him, fairly sure he was being modest. "Well—cloak or no cloak, it fits." She smiled, the effort shy. "I—I just wanted to say, I'm sorry about being so short with you because of your disapproving attitude about Perrier." She looked down at her clenched hands, feeling his eyes on her. "My father hated animals. Your critical tone reminded me..."

The wool fabric of his suit whispered against the chair as he shifted. She could tell by the creak of leather and the subtle hint of aftershave as he leaned closer. "Then please forgive me for my critical tone. It was uncalled for."

It took a man of exceptional self-confidence to ask someone's forgiveness when it wasn't necessary. She flicked her gaze up to tell him so, but was struck by the imposing sight. He'd turned more fully in her direction and rested a forearm on the table. He looked quite debonair, impeccably dressed in black, his blood-red tie a vibrant contrast to his starched, white shirt. Precisely correct cuffs showed beyond his suit-sleeves; custom-made, hammered gold cuff links sparkled in the beam of the reading light above his head. Lassiter Dragan was a man of quiet power, exuding vitality, confidence and a discerning sense of taste.

She couldn't bring herself to voice the fact that he owed her no apology. She had trouble finding words, so she nodded and smiled her thanks. "Well—I'll just go back to my seat. Perrier might get frightened if I'm gone too long."

"Perrier," he repeated with that wry, half smile. "A fancy French word for a fancy French poodle?"

"Oh, no," Trisha said. "Perrier's not a fancy anything. I told you I found her abandoned on the side of the road, and that's not where fancy French poodles come from." With a melancholy smile, she recalled the day she found Perrier. "The vet and I figured out that she's half poodle and half terrier. I guess the owner of the purebred mother dog decided to dump the worthless mixed breed puppies."

She sighed, unable to understand such cruel callousness. "I rescued three of Perrier's brothers and sisters that had been dumped along with her, and eventually found them homes. Anyway, since she's part terrier and part poodle, I exchanged the T in terrier for the P in poodle and named her Perrier in honor of her mama and papa. I pronounce it like the fancy French water, but that's the only fancy thing about her."

Trisha glanced in the direction where her pet slept. "To me, her pedigree is one hundred percent angel."

"I see," he said.

She shifted her attention to him, experiencing that prick of disappointment again. His eyes were beautiful, but they exhibited only steely, cool civility. "No, you don't, Mr. Dragan." She sucked in a breath, reminding herself it wasn't her job to be the world's conscience. "But you have a right not to."

His eyebrows dipped slightly, as though he didn't quite get it, but his half grin remained intact. "Thank you, Miss August."

"You're welcome, Mr. Dragan." She smiled, the expression less happy than well-intentioned. *I will not lecture or judge!* she cautioned inwardly. *I've been given a great opportunity, and I will not blow it by picking a fight with my benefactor—no matter how misguided he is.*

When Trisha stepped out of Lassiter's jet, she was surprised it was cold in Las Vegas. Though the temperature wasn't quite freezing, she had always pictured the desert city as perpetually hot. Apparently, even a desert oasis like Las Vegas, with all its manmade glitz and glamour was not immune from the changing seasons.

A hired limousine was there to drive them to their hotel. Trisha spent the short trip clutching Perrier protectively to her and looking out the window at bright lights in the distance. She checked her wristwatch. Nine-fifteen. The pilot had mentioned they'd crossed two time zones, so in Las Vegas it must be seven-fifteen. That was almost the same time the Dragan jet had taken off from Kansas City's International airport. The fact that two hours had just disappeared seemed remarkable. She turned to mention it to her host who sat next to her in the back seat. He was on his cell phone, dictating a letter to his secretary's voice mail. It seemed business, for him, was a twenty-four-hour-a-day obsession.

Instead of remarking on the time, she turned away and reset her watch, deciding she was lucky he was too busy for her to talk to. A man with his own jet was obviously accustomed to crossing time zones. Her amazement would have sounded ignorant to him.

She felt strangely alone, but not so alone she couldn't detect his presence. Though they weren't touching, she could feel his warmth. His aftershave was a heady breathing experience. She sensed, as far as he was concerned, she might as well be invisible. It was hard to get used to the idea of taking a trip with a man in the first place. But it was harder to get it straight in her head that she was no more significant to him than his shoes—necessary but certainly not special.

The ride wasn't long, but seemed like an eternity. When she stepped out of the limo, she gaped at their hotel. She'd heard that Las Vegas boasted some of the world's most spectacular hotels, but The Monarch was an architectural masterpiece of solid glass walls, accented by a glass and brass revolving door, marble floors, stunning fountains, sweeping arches and chandeliered domes.

The beaming, chatty desk clerk referred to The Monarch's location as "the most exciting corner in the country, overlooking the gaming capital of the world." Trisha was surprised by how little the grinning man had exaggerated, for when she was ushered into the penthouse suite, she was immediately overwhelmed by the sweeping vistas beyond the floor-to-ceiling windows.

On one side, daylight reigned, from their view of the hotels on the Strip, a dazzling show of pulsating lights and an endless sea of humanity. The other direction was like a completely different planet. It was dark, bathed only in moonlight, all natural and quiet. In the distance, a majestic, snow-covered mountain dominated.

"What's that?" she asked the porter.

The swarthy, mustachioed man glanced in the direction she pointed. "It's Mt. Charleston, ma'am. Over 11,000 feet high." He jerked his head off to her left. "Bedrooms are back that way. Where would you like the bags?"

"Oh…" She had no idea, and Lassiter seemed to have disappeared. "Just leave them there." She bit her lip. The young man needed a tip, didn't he? She grabbed her purse and fished inside for some money. She'd brought along twenty-three dollars, all she had in her apartment. Pulling out the three singles she held them out, hoping it was enough. "Here, and thanks."

The porter shook his head. "The Mister took care of me, ma'am." He smiled. "If you need anything, I'm George." He gave a jaunty salute and spun on his heel, heading crisply toward the door.

She stood like a statue until the sound of the door closing snapped her out of her stupor. Well, it was nice of Mr. Dragan to take care of the tip—before he disappeared.

She sighed, glancing around. The gracious entry foyer led into a spacious living room and an elegant dining room, with seating for eight, and a view of both the strip and the mountains. With its Victorian decor, it seemed more like those houses you saw in fancy home decorating magazines than a hotel suite—with etched mirrors, richly hued wallpaper, oil paintings and glittering chandeliers. She took a slow walking tour of the place. The bedrooms, too, were impressively furnished with what looked like *real* artwork and *real* antiquities. But she was no expert. As she went around opening doors, she discovered to her astonishment, that each bedroom had its own lavish, marble bathroom. What luxury!

Exhilarated and agitated, she couldn't relax, couldn't even sit down, so she walked outside, through a set of French doors. She found herself on the hotel roof, which served as the penthouse's terrace. Off to her right she was stunned to find an Olympic size pool, inlaid with marble. It was enclosed inside a waist-high, wrought-iron fence. She couldn't believe her eyes, but when she walked over to lean against the fence, she could smell chlorine. A swimming pool on a roof! Lit from underwater, it fairly glowed in the darkness like a blue gemstone.

A haze rose from the surface, a telltale sign that it was heated for year-round enjoyment. "Of course it's heated," she said with a laugh, to Perrier, cuddled in her arms. "We must have our December dip or the holidays wouldn't be complete."

She moved to the chest-high rail that surrounded the terrace's edge and peered over. Below their fortieth story suite, the grounds were lushly landscaped with a sparkling water environment, surrounded by exotic trees and vegetation. The sound of a rushing waterfall rose up to the penthouse, a low, restful rumble. Gas-lit promenades meandered in the dense foliage, at times teasing the water's edge then dipping into deep shadows, the perfect environment for romantic walks and tantalizing trysts for honeymooning lovers.

Trisha experienced a shiver, recalling why she was in Las Vegas—to *pretend* to be one of those honeymooning lovers. She swallowed hard. Lassiter Dragan, pulse-pounding handsome and wealthy beyond her wildest imaginings, would be on any normal female's wish list as a honeymoon lover. And there she was—*with him*—but not really with him.

Experiencing a confusing mix of emotions, she turned away from the rail and walked to the French doors. With her hand on the knob, she paused to look inside. She felt like she shouldn't go in, that she didn't belong there. Suddenly, she was the little match girl standing in the cold, watching a happy family enjoy Christmas turkey before a glowing hearth.

"But there's no happy family enjoying Christmas turkey inside," she murmured. "No hearth glows. Even my pretend bridegroom is nowhere to be found." She wondered where he was and if he would even share the suite with her.

Deciding she was being silly to cower outside like some stray kitten, she opened the doors and walked in. Looking around, she was once again amazed by the opulence in which some people lived. The suite was as big as a house. Certainly more room than any two people who were only spending the weekend needed. She could have fit her one-room garage apartment in here ten times.

After making the rounds twice more, she set Perrier on the floor and dropped onto a bed to stare unseeing out of a large window, at the moonlit, snow-covered mountain. She liked this view best. It was not only beautiful, and so unlike Kansas City, but it was peaceful, calming.

"There you are," came a deep, male voice.

Trisha jumped and twisted around to see Lassiter in the bedroom doorway. So much for peace and calm.

"I thought I'd lost you," he said.

"I've been here all the time," she said.

"Meaning, I haven't." Once again he seemed to read her mind. "I ran into an acquaintance."

"The pretty woman in the lobby who dropped her purse?"

He leaned against the door jamb. "Yeah." He indicated the room. "Will this do for you?"

Apparently that was the end of the "pretty woman" discussion. She supposed any man as good-looking as Lassiter Dragan would be in danger of running into women, whether they were past acquaintances or not, who would drop purses, handkerchiefs, bracelets, shoes, socks, even *underwear,* simply to get his attention.

"Is there a problem with the room?" he asked.

She realized she must have been frowning. "Oh—no." Getting her mind on track, she took in the luxurious furnishings, from the extensively carved four-poster bed with its azure, brocade spread to the wonderful antique writing desk. She especially loved the room-size, intricately woven Oriental rug. Trisha turned her attention to her host. "I'd be pretty picky if it didn't do."

"Fine." He loosened his tie, the act uncommonly sexy, considering he was only trying to get more comfortable. "I'll take the last bedroom down the hall. Since I'll be making business calls, I don't want to keep you awake."

She nodded, understanding all too well. He also wouldn't want her to get any misguided notions about why she was here, and why he was going to all this bother. Certainly not out of any heated fantasies about her.

She made a production of yawning, telling herself it was not a self-deluded effort to shore up her pride. She was, after all, getting her business loan. Just because Mr. Dragan was tormentingly handsome didn't change the basic deal they'd agreed to. "Excuse me," she said, patting her mouth. "I am tired."

"Before I forget," he said, "I've hired a car for you for

tomorrow. The chauffeur has been instructed to pick you up at ten and drive you to the best Las Vegas apparel stores. From what I've seen of your clothes today, I don't think I need to fear that you'll use bad judgment in purchasing appropriate clothes. But if you have any questions, ask a salesclerk.''

She experienced a stab of indignation. She hadn't realized how much of a hick he believed her to be until this minute. At least that cleared up the mystery of why he'd chosen her for this magazine prank—because they were from different worlds. After the holidays, when she was running her discount doggie boutique and he was back in the stratosphere of society, they would never again see each other. There social stations were too far apart. He'd be in no danger of an embarrassing reminder.

''Why—thank you *ever* so much for the shopping tip!'' She rose to face him. Ignoring the voice in her head screaming at her to keep her big mouth shut, she went on, her smile tight, ''And I'll come straight to *you* if I have any questions about how to behave like a pompous ass!''

The effect of her sarcasm was a graveyard stillness. Yet as hushed as the world around her had become, inside her head her insult echoed—too loud and too clear.

Now you've done it, Trisha! she scolded silently. *Was it really necessary to call him on his conceit? For one thing, you can kiss that loan goodbye. In about a minute, he's going to boot you out of this swanky hotel, and you and Perrier will have a nice, long stroll back to Kansas City!*

''I have never—in my life...'' he began slowly, his expression less than cheerful.

Here it comes! The big boot! A knot of anxiety twisted in her stomach, but she kept her head high. After all, he *had* been condescending! He *had* insulted her! *That's just fine and dandy!* The voice in her head jeered, *but you're about to pay a devastating price for your righteous indignation!*

''...ever apologized to the same person twice in a single day,'' he said. No longer leaning against the door jamb, he stood erect, framed in the doorway—a Greek god in a five-thousand dollar suit.

He dipped his head slightly in what looked like a nod of deference. "I didn't mean to insult you, Miss August. I hope you can forgive me for my thoughtlessness."

What did he say? she quizzed herself. It hadn't sounded like *"Get out!"* She stared in disbelief. He'd actually apologized to her—again? She didn't know how to react. He was unquestionably true to the distinction as "Gentleman Dragon." She studied him, confused. After a time, it occurred to her that he looked awfully cool and casual in his repentance.

At long last the truth hit and her confusion dissipated like steam on a cooling latte. How could she have been such a dullard not to have seen it before? "I believe you meant that, Mr. Dragan," she said. "Thank you. But tell me," she went on, "Have you ever been really sorry?"

His eyebrows dipped at her query. "I beg your pardon?"

She crossed her arms before her, feeling like she was on to something. "I mean have you ever had your heart broken? Mourned an all-consuming loss? Been so lost and alone you didn't care if tomorrow came or not?"

He watched her curiously. "Everyone has losses."

"Yes, but have you ever had a loss you could never get over? One that broke you into little pieces, and you haven't been whole since?"

He shifted his attention away, seeming to look inward. "No," he said after a pause, then met her gaze again. "I suppose not."

She absorbed that news. "What about great joy?" she asked. "Have you ever felt so happy you could almost burst with it?"

His lips curved in a cynical half smile. "I gather we're not talking about great sex?"

She stifled a gasp, but could do nothing about her hot blush. "No," she said. "Seriously. Have you ever known great, earth-shattering joy?"

He slipped his hands into his trouser pockets, his manner detached. "What's your point, Miss August?"

She shrugged and sat down on the bed. "I was deciding how heartfelt your apologies really are." She waited expectantly for his next question to come. The one where he would ask, *"And just how heartfelt do you believe they are?"*

He smiled smoothly, revealing nothing of his thoughts. "Good night, Miss August." He grasped the crystal knob and shut the door between them.

CHAPTER FIVE

TRISHA felt like a princess in a fairy story. She'd spent all day shopping for clothes, and not just dresses, tops and trousers, either. She'd purchased lovely underthings, a negligee, even shoes and handbags. She'd never been so coordinated in her life. She'd never even thought about being so coordinated.

Every item she'd acquired had been seriously luxurious, in fabric and design, all too beautiful for words. Trisha hadn't dreamed of owning clothes like these, but if smart, sleek, comfortable elegance was the image her *pretend* husband wanted her to project, she was ready to oblige.

She looked at herself in the full length mirror in her spacious, rose-marble bathroom. She'd chosen a delicious, cashmere trousers set to show off to Mr. Dragan—white, full-leg trousers and a body-hugging, cowl neck sweater. To add a splash of color, she decided to wear a Christmas wreath pin, made of colored chips of glass, that she'd brought from home. It had belonged to her mother, wasn't elegant, was never meant to be. But to Trisha it was as much a part of Christmas as the turkey dinner, singing carols or decorating the tree.

In honor of her mother's memory, she fastened the pin to her cowl collar and checked the results in the mirror. She liked the effect of the sparkling green and red Christmas wreath against the snowy sweater. All in all, her sporty ensemble fit her figure beautifully, exuding comfortable luxury. "So this is what expensive clothes can do?" She touched her mother's Christmas pin fondly, hoping it looked as fitting on the expensive sweater as she thought it did. "Just give it one, negative squint, Mr. Dragan," she dared him under her breath. "And I'll blacken one of your sexy eyes!"

She still smarted from his arrogance. "I don't think I need to *fear* that you'll use bad judgment in purchasing appropriate clothes," she mimicked in an uppity tone. That stuffy remark had been burned so strongly in her memory she hadn't asked a single, solitary saleslady for an opinion. It was a matter of pride. She might not have buckets of money, but she had perfectly fine taste. "He'd better not find fault!" she said so forcefully Perrier raised her head inquiringly.

"Sorry, sweetie, I didn't mean to sound mad." She smiled at her pet, curled on the bathroom rug. "I don't blame you for liking that rug. It's so soft, I think it's made of clouds. You finish your nap."

Perrier yawned and lowered her head, clearly deciding the fluffy rug was vacation enough for her.

Trisha walked out of the bath, trying to put Mr. Dragan's condescension behind her. After all, today she'd charged thousands of dollars worth of new clothes to his account, not to mention the fifty-thousand dollar loan he'd promised. Nothing was perfect, so how close to it did she need to get to be happy?

She slipped into white, suede ankle boots, and with a deep breath, left her bedroom. Though the penthouse suite was large, space shared with the studly Lassiter Dragan seemed overcrowded. She'd especially noticed it when she'd returned from shopping an hour ago, and caught him coming inside after a swim in the pool. She wondered how she could have felt so oxygen-deprived in a place that opened out to a rooftop veranda with a vast sky overhead. During the thirty seconds it took him to pass by with a brief nod, and stroll to his bedroom, she'd hardly been able to catch her breath.

Rounding the corner into the living room, she heard Lassiter before she saw him. He was talking business, the conversation punctuated with catchwords and phrases like "high-growth," "return on investment," "IPO" and "target market." Her glance went toward the sound of his voice. He sat on one of the two ruby silk sofas, facing each other, in front of a stone fireplace,

He wore jeans and a navy turtleneck sweater that looked comfortable and warm. His boots were the lace-up kind, like you'd see on construction workers or serious hikers. She was surprised by his ultra casual clothes, making him look more like the boy next door than a jet-set corporate icon.

In the hearth, flames licked at a stack of hardwood; its smoky aroma drifted across the air, a homey touch she hadn't expected.

Uncertain about what to do, she came to a stop. She didn't want to make undue noise that might break his train of thought. Considering the kind of money he worked with, a badly timed cough might kill a multimillion dollar deal.

He noticed her and motioned her over. She experienced an unexpected flutter in her breast and obeyed with a smile, amazed at how swiftly any harbored hostility could dissipate with Lassiter Dragan's most casual eye contact. She experienced a surge of hope that he would notice her outfit, possibly even compliment her.

He shifted on the couch, removing something from his jeans pocket. Whatever he held, it was too small for Trisha to see. "It's an excellent opportunity, Bill," he said into the receiver, making a "come closer" motion.

She stepped around the coffee table separating the two sofas, and moved close enough to reach out and touch him. He startled her by taking her left hand and lifting it toward him. The unexpected contact sent a thrill zinging along her spine. "Bill, it's important to bring the technology to market ahead of the previously predicted adoption curve, and at accessible price points," he said. During a pause, he slipped something on her ring finger. "Absolutely," he went on, releasing her. "We capitalize on the full potential." His expression was concentrated, his attention elsewhere. Whatever the reason he'd called her over, had ceased to exist.

She remained standing as she had when he'd held her hand. Glancing down, she stared at the fingers he'd abruptly abandoned. A flash on her ring finger caught her attention. What in heaven's name was that? It looked like two gold bands, one plain, one sporting an oval diamond the size of a coffee bean.

She stared in disbelief. Lassiter Dragan had just slipped a wedding set on her finger—and he hadn't even interrupted a phone call to do it. He hadn't lost the thread of his conversation. He hadn't even looked at her when he'd put the rings on her finger.

The act couldn't have been more destitute of emotion. *Well, what did you expect?* she berated inwardly, *Hearts and flowers? A romantic dinner and a proposal on bended knee? The wedding set is part of his ploy. Just because he's exciting to look at without his shirt—and with it—and just because charisma gushes off him like water over Niagara Falls, and just because the diamond is real, don't forget—the marriage is not!*

When she noticed her throat had gone dry, she grasped the fact that she'd been standing there with her mouth open for heaven knew how long. *"Oh—my...."* she murmured.

"Excuse me, Bill." Her host shifted his attention to her, his expression inquiring. "Did you say something?"

She stared, wide-eyed for a second, then shook her head. "Uh—no..." Holding out the hand with the rings, she cleared her throat. "It's—pretty." *What a world-class understatement.*

His glance flicked over the rings. "Do they fit?"

She nodded. "Like they were..." She stopped herself. The rings had *not* been meant for her. "I mean—yes."

"Good." He continued to watch her for a few seconds. "Was there anything else you wanted?"

A heaviness centered in her chest, but she kept her features composed. "No—nothing."

He nodded. "Dinner should be here shortly."

"Fine." She took a step backward, the weirdest sensation of disappointment settling in her stomach like a lead weight. The reaction was so foolish she was annoyed with herself. "I'll get the door when it comes." She hoped she could eat.

"Thanks. I'm back, Bill." His gaze and his attention withdrew from her. She could feel it disconnect, like a supporting girder, and she teetered unsteadily. "As I was saying," he went on, his voice authoritative, "they have a growing patent portfolio, with wide-ranging product development, OEM and licensing opportunities." He stared thoughtfully into space, his brow creased as he listened. "No, you're missing the point."

He ran a hand through his hair, mussing it pleasantly. "No, no, listen to me, Bill."

Feeling like a dismissed child, Trisha watched him for another moment from the safety of her invisibility to this man. She noticed he wore a ring, too—a wide, golden band. It made sense that he would provide himself with a wedding ring. They *were* supposed to be married.

When she realized she was staring, practically *mooning* over the man, she pivoted away and hurried to the window wall. It was as far away as she could get from her fake husband, and still be available to answer the door when room service brought their dinner.

She stared out at the Las Vegas Strip, pulsating with light and life. She loved to people-watch, so she decided to put everything out of her mind except the tourists bustling along the thoroughfare below. She tried, for long minutes she tried, but her fake husband's face kept looming in her mind's eye.

"I'm sorry about all the phone calls."

Trisha almost jumped out of her skin at the sound of his voice, so close behind her.

"Oh…" She whirled around. "You walk softly."

He grinned that noncommittal, half grin. "Sorry."

She knew he was teasing her with another neutral apology that meant nothing, so her answering smile was cynical. "No—no—it's—entirely—my—fault," she said, her tone mechanical.

He surveyed her, still grinning, and for a second she thought it reached his eyes. "I'm honestly sorry about being on the phone so much. Something came up that needs to be settled by Monday."

"Is it settled?"

He crossed his arms over his chest. "That's the eternal question."

Unaccustomed to wearing jewelry, she found herself twisting the wedding set around her finger. Since the rings were on her mind, she lifted her hand to admire them. "Are these family heirlooms?"

He glanced at her hand. "Yes. They're my great-grandmother's on my mother's side."

"And yours?" She indicated his wedding band.

"My great-grandfather's."

"How lucky you had wedding rings lying around."

"More like inevitable, with a family motto that goes, 'Acquire, acquire then acquire more.'"

"Oh, right." The reminder was sobering. "I forgot who I was talking to." She examined the lovely set on her finger, sparkling in reflected light from the Strip. After a second of contemplation, she asked, "How would your great-grandmother feel if she knew an impostor bride would one day wear her wedding rings?"

"I doubt that it was at the top of her wish list," he admitted. "But having them melted down into a gaudy tie tack would be even less desirable, I'm sure."

"Would you do that?" she asked, troubled by the idea.

He shook his head, the act as much a rebuke as a no. "Didn't you catch the word 'gaudy'?"

His taunt pricked her pride. "Oh, yes—you're the Lord High Chancellor of deciding what is *appropriate* and what isn't."

He regarded her impassively, her baiting apparently having no effect. He touched her wreath pin, ran a finger around it. Though the contact was light and brief, she couldn't breathe.

"You brought this with you?"

She managed to nod, but her adrenaline level rose. *One wrong word, Mr. Dragan, and you're toast!* she warned silently.

He skimmed his finger along the bridge of her nose, the gentleness of the act out of sync with anything she would have expected from such an emotionally detached man. She experienced an electrical shock at the contact. Self-conscious about that bump, she placed a protective hand over the place he'd touched. "Why did you do that?" The question came out panicky, which had *not* been her intention.

Never taking his eyes off her, he slipped his hands into his jeans pockets. "How did you break it?" he asked.

His bluntness made her cheeks sizzle. "In a neighborhood baseball game when I was eleven," she said, the recollection distressing. "I was next up to the plate, and the hitter threw her bat. It smacked me in the nose." She rubbed the lump before making herself drop her hand. So she had a bump on her nose. It was nothing to be ashamed about. "Mother said it gave my face character," she murmured, unable to hold eye contact.

When he didn't respond, she experienced a nagging, swelling defiance, and couldn't help but meet his gaze. "Well—maybe there are people who'll read the magazine article who have bumps on their noses, too, and they'll see mine and feel compelled to give you their business!" she blurted. "Try to think of it that way!" Agitated, she glared.

His brow creased. "Don't be so defensive, Miss August. Your nose is fine. It could be a veritable shrine to character, and it would still be a very appealing nose." With a nod toward her wreath pen, he added, "That's a nice touch of color, by the way."

Nerves that had been stretched to the breaking point went slack, the effect so sudden she almost collapsed. He'd actually said the crooked protrusion on her face was appealing. And he'd complimented her cheap, glass Christmas wreath pin. She didn't think she betrayed her surprise and relief with more than a few extra blinks. At least she hoped not. It wouldn't do to let him know his opinion could propel her into the stratosphere or crush her into the ground, the way it apparently could. She must work on her "aloofness" skills where this man was concerned.

She lifted her chin, hoping she exhibited cool dignity. "Oh—well…thank you."

"You're welcome," he said. "You look lovely. Or did you think I hadn't noticed?"

"I—I…why, it never crossed my mind!" she lied, her disobedient pulse rate tripling in tempo. "I hope you think my shopping spree was worth it when you get the bill."

"It will be. The *Urban Sophisticate* article is worth millions to me in free advertising," he said.

She sucked in a breath. "Millions of—*dollars?*" She knew he'd said the article would be good for his business, but *millions* good? She couldn't even compute that in her mind.

"Millions of dollars, yes."

"But—aren't you already filthy rich?" she asked. "I mean—how many millions will it take before you're satisfied?"

"Define satisfied."

The tension that had momentarily eased was building, again. She could feel it in the increased rate of her breathing and the noise of her heart thudding in her ears. She didn't like the direction of their conversation. It upset her on a gut level she couldn't comprehend. "Preoccupation with money is the great test of small natures, but only a small test of great ones," she said. "Sébastien-Roch Nicolas de Chamfor, said that, and I believe it's true."

"Did your Mr. Chamfor define 'satisfied'?" He placed the flat of one hand against the window near her shoulder, and she backed into the cold glass. He was too close. The scent of his cologne was too stimulating, his lips too alluring. Why did she feel a wayward urge to throw herself into his arms?

His intense, sleepy-lidded gaze sent a surge of longing rampaging through her. She reminded herself that this marriage ploy was a business arrangement. *Purely business!* So why this sudden, wild desire to make their pact anything *but* pure. "Money can't buy happiness, Mr. Dragan!" She gulped in a great draught of air to clear her head.

"But money lets you look for happiness in a lot of nice places."

A chill dashed down Trisha's spine. How many times had she heard her father say the same thing? Suddenly the idea of spending two weeks with the luscious Lassiter Dragan became a disgraceful travesty. From the first instant she'd met him, she'd been drawn to the man. But now, like a sharp slap, she faced a truth she'd begun to sense with his initial, negative reaction to Perrier.

Lassiter Dragan was the same self-centered, success-obsessed breed as her father!

The fairy tale dissolved, disappeared, and she mentally hauled out all her defenses. She wasn't stupid. She wouldn't walk out on their deal. Nobody ever accused Trisha August of being the type to cut off her nose to spite her face—no matter how bumpy or crooked it was.

Men like Mr. Dragan and her father might be flesh and blood, human beings, but they lacked some vital chromosomes. Bred out of them, in their single-minded quest for wealth, were the warm, caring qualities a woman needed from the man she loved. Any crazy illusions Trisha may have dreamed up about The Gentleman Dragon being a modern-day Prince Charming had to be stomped to dust.

"In all that white, you look like a bride."

The word "bride" jolted her, and she grew alarmed. Only a moment ago she'd actually fantasized about…well, that was then! Before reality kicked her hard in the belly. Lassiter Dragan was a calculating, money-hungry opportunist exactly like her father.

"Which is a subject we need to discuss."

"Discuss?" she asked, distrustful and confused.

He nodded, watching her with brilliant, penetrating eyes that missed nothing, yet were strangely veiled, keeping those who tried to read *his* thoughts, judge *his* mood, locked outside. Even the smile on his lips could be a ruse, a disguise, beyond which no man or woman could penetrate, never to know precisely how much happiness or humor he truly felt—if any. Or if the charming facade of The Gentleman Dragon, hid a man devoid of human emotion.

She shook off the irrational thought. That was impossible. By nature, man was a creature of emotion, made of flesh and blood and bone. He bled and broke, laughed and cried, loved and lost. Mr. Lassiter Dragan might be better than most at governing his emotions, or hiding them, but he had to feel.

What are you doing, waxing poetic about this man? she asked herself. *After the holidays you'll never see him again, so why dwell on his hidden emotional life?*

Determined not to allow his closeness to intimidate her, she tried to recall what they'd been discussing. They'd been discussing *discussing* something. Staring into those mysterious, silvery eyes, she experienced a rush of overheated awareness. "What—what did you want to discuss?" she asked. Was he closer than he'd been a moment ago? Or was his charisma so potent the space around him seemed to shrink?

He grinned, a cavalier flash of teeth. "I've decided we should get married."

CHAPTER SIX

THE "discussion" was brief and one-sided. A minister was summoned and the ceremony accomplished swiftly and without fanfare. Not even a kiss. Trisha told herself that was perfectly fine. She had no intention of falling in love with Lassiter Dragan. She had no intention of even falling in *lust* with him. Kisses were dangerous things to fool around with, and Trisha sensed Mr. Dragan's—that is, *her husband's*—kisses might be a little too much like peanuts. Impossible to walk away from after just one.

As soon as the nuptial papers were signed, Lassiter ushered out the minister and the two bellboys who served as witnesses. Once again alone with Lassiter, it hit her. She was *Mrs. Lassiter Dragan*. She stood there, mutely, feeling no different. Maybe a little let down and unsure why. Her deal was the same, the only change was the marriage was no longer a lie, but a precautionary safeguard, in case some nosy news hound checked it out. And, of course, the fifty thousand dollar loan would be hers, at prime, the moment she signed their annulment papers. It was all so practical and legal and devoid of messy emotions.

Now that it was done, Trisha couldn't fathom how he'd talked her into an actual marriage. But Lassiter had a soft-spoken way about him that clearly had a dangerously hypnotic effect. As he'd made his case, it sounded so simple, even necessary. He'd explained, if the ruse were discovered before the article came out, the story would be canceled, and "all this" would have been for nothing. If the ruse were discovered after the article, and the truth hit the news, his life would once again become a living hell, as it had after the first article—all those crazy females invading his privacy, bringing business to a

70

standstill. She could understand why he couldn't let that happen.

He'd assured her, she would also be better served if they were actually married. Trisha had to admit, she was conservative enough to prefer that people think she and Mr. Dragan had fallen madly, insanely into a love that burned hot and incendiary for a brief time, then as quickly flickered out. That was more palatable than the vision of friends snickering behind her back about how she'd foolishly run off and had a quickie affair, becoming just another notch on a rich playboy's bedpost.

She couldn't imagine what her mother would have thought. She probably wouldn't have called it Trisha's most shining moment. But, since the marriage was purely a precaution, and wouldn't compromise her principles, and since she was on the verge of realizing her dream, a business of her own, she prayed her mother would have understood.

Now their Las Vegas weekend looked exactly like it was— a *genuine* quickie wedding and honeymoon. Apart from Saturday's shopping spree, the couple passed their entire stay in seclusion in their penthouse suite, exactly like impassioned newlyweds—except for the impassioned part.

At noon on Monday, December twenty-fourth, they flew back to Kansas City. The plane ride was silent and strained. Trisha was agitated almost to the point of hysteria. She knew they should be perfecting their story, but she couldn't bring herself to begin a conversation. Lassiter worked at his computer, looking cross. She feared his moodiness had more to do with her than business worries. Well, drat the man! He had nobody to be angry with but himself. The ploy had been his idea. He'd made his marriage bed, let him sulk in it!

The chauffeur was at the airport when their plane landed. Trisha's newly acquired wardrobe went into the limousine, since the huge stack of boxes didn't have a prayer of fitting into Mr. Dragan's sports car. Trisha rode with her new husband in the sporty two-seater, as a bride would be expected to do—just in case the magazine people arrived early. Once again, she was thrust into a "too-close-for-comfort" situation.

He smelled so good in the confined space. And every time he shifted gears, his arm grazed hers. Even through her coat, the effect was troublingly erotic.

They rode in silence for over half an hour. Trisha was tense, her only calming outlet, petting Perrier, napping in her lap. After a while she realized they cruised along a blacktop road amid stands of evergreens and oaks, blanketed in white. Bare, stark branches of elm and maple trees stretched upward toward a heavy, overcast sky that heralded more snow.

Moments later, they came to a ten-foot wall of gray limestone. Lassiter Dragan pulled to a stop before an imposing, wrought iron gate, its two sections slowly parting to grant them entry. Trisha thought of what he'd said about women throwing themselves on his car, after the last published magazine article about him. It must have been quite a scene. She contemplated the sports car's cloth roof. "Did you have this car when the women mobbed you here?" She bit her tongue, flustered. She hadn't meant to ask that aloud.

He flicked her a glance, then returned his attention to accelerating through the gate. "Why?" He skimmed along a narrow drive that wound through the trees on his vast grounds.

Trisha swallowed, feeling foolish. She lowered her gaze to Perrier. "I just wondered if they damaged your car's cloth top."

He maneuvered around a bend. "That was five years ago." She felt his gaze rest briefly on her. "Since this Porsche is new, I gather you're not a sports car fan."

"I don't own a car," she said. "And I don't know one kind from another." She stared out of her side window, better to avoid looking at him. He was a heart-racing sight in a sky-blue, cable-knit turtleneck and jeans. Why did he dress in clothes that *magnified* his broad shoulders, trim waist and taut... She winced, making herself scan the snowy lawn, untouched by tracks of any kind. Along the way, they passed terraced, landscaped berms of plantings, no doubt stunning when green and blooming. "It's not my lack of enthusiasm for cars," she went on, trying not to picture him in her mind. "I can't afford one."

She glanced forward but couldn't see the house. She wondered how much property Lassiter Dragan owned, but clamped her jaws, refusing to ask. She peeked his way, took in his wonderful profile, his sharp, breath-stealing features. Her chest grew tight. Condemning herself silently for her lapse, she turned away, glanced down. The sparkle of a diamond caught her eye and she stared at the wedding set on her left hand. "I wonder what your great-grandmother would think, now," she mused aloud. "We're married, but it's still a dishonorable fraud."

He didn't speak. She looked up. His jaw bunched as though he were gritting his teeth.

"That thrilled, huh?" Trisha wondered if his discomfort was merely annoyance for the jab about his great-grandmother, or if he felt a prick of conscience. Since he was a younger version of her father—worshiping the almighty dollar—she had to go with her first notion. Lassiter was annoyed with her, nothing more.

Around another bend, beyond a dense stand of snowy pin oaks, she glimpsed, at last, Lassiter Dragan's home. It unfolded gradually, appearing to grow out of the landscape.

She was surprised by its distinctive Spanish flavor. Beneath an age-mellowed terra-cotta tile roof, the windows were deep-set. Horizontally stacked blocks of limestone formed solid, thick walls. Brickwork around picturesque arches added impact. A much larger, more dramatic archway sheltered the home's entry beyond a gated courtyard.

Trisha was impressed, and though she vowed to remain emotionally aloof, she felt the need to say so. "You have a beautiful home, Mr. Dragan."

"Thank you—Mrs. Dragan." He pulled the car to a stop before the entry arch, shifting to face her. "Now that we're home, call me Lassiter—or, preferably, darling." She must have looked shocked, because he shook his head, his brow creased with aggravation. "It was merely a suggestion. You may call me anything you're comfortable with. Except Mr. Dragan, of course." He turned off the engine. "I've decided to call you sweetheart. It has a simple, affectionate ring to it."

It was her turn to feel aggravated. She smiled perversely. "Not to mention, if my name slips your mind, it won't matter."

His expression darkened, the silence chilling. Or was the frigidity in the air merely the north wind seeping into the car now that the heat was off? "Yes," he said, finally. "That's true." Turning away, he unlatched his door and climbed out.

"Yes? That's true?" she muttered, wondering why his response bothered her. After all, she'd brought it up. Her car door clicked open and she swiveled around to see Lassiter standing there, broad-shouldered and luscious. He extended a hand.

She didn't like the idea of accepting his help out, but with Perrier clutched in her arms, her exit from the low bucket seat would be awkward. Before she could argue herself out of it, some perverse need made her accept Lassiter's extended fingers. "Why, thank you—my darling—*cockatrice.*"

"Your darling what?" he asked.

"Cockatrice. It's a serpent hatched from a cock's egg, with the power to kill at a glance." Safely out of the car and standing beside him, she pulled from his grip to resettle Perrier in both arms. "That's what I've decided to call you." In her whole life, Trisha had hardly made a more ridiculous statement. But the touch of his hand had been too warm, too welcome. That unsettled her, made her mad at herself. It wasn't his fault he affected her so strongly, but she decided to take it out on him with the only power she had—the choice he'd given her.

He frowned. "You're kidding."

She found his displeasure satisfying. "Serpent—Dragon? Get it?" she asked. "I read a lot and pick up interesting trivia."

"Apparently."

She felt invigorated, relished wielding her power. She would exact a bit of revenge for the times he'd nonchalantly backed her into corners. "You said I could call you anything I was comfortable with," she reminded him. "'Cockatrice' fits you."

To Trisha, the idea of calling anybody "cockatrice" was absurd, but that wasn't the point. Her power to touch him, affect him, was what mattered. She had no plans to make him suffer very long. She only wanted a moment of fun.

He wasn't smiling any of his emotionless, noncommittal smiles now. "Cockatrice sounds like cockroach." He indicated the gated archway that led into a courtyard. "Why not call me 'my darling' and leave off the part that *fits*."

"Well…" She pretended to ponder his suggestion. If she were to be honest, calling this man "my darling" would be easy. Too easy.

"Why does it fit me?" he asked, as they walked beneath the deep archway that housed a room above it.

Trisha looked up, guessing it must be visitor's quarters.

"Did you hear me?" he asked, sounding put out. Did her opinion matter, or was he simply so accustomed to being obeyed, he refused to accept a hint of rebellion even in such a trifling matter?

"Yes—I heard. I was just—never mind." She sensed his patience wearing thin. Her teasing couldn't go on much longer. "Well, besides the serpent-dragon connection, it fits you because you have lethal eyes." That was too true. "They're silvery—steely, really. Sharp as a dagger. They're cockatrice eyes if I ever saw them." As she preceded him through the gate into a courtyard, she didn't add that his eyes were also too sexy to bear.

They walked in silence across a stone patio. Though it was swept clear of snowdrifts, they were surrounded by white ghosts of garden plantings, shrubs and ornamental trees, framing windows and accenting the massive, carved double-doored entry.

"I'd prefer 'darling,'" he said. "Or 'my darling.'"

She glanced his way. "I'm not comfortable with that," she objected, truly reluctant. But she couldn't tell him *why*—that "my darling" would flow too easily off her tongue. "You promised I could be comfortable with whatever I chose."

"Not at my expense," he said, flatly.

Her foray into power fizzled, but she refused to let it die.

If he wanted her to play the part of his wife, she had power whether he liked it or not. "I see," she said, crisply. "My comfort hangs on *your* comfort. Why didn't you say so—Mr. Dragan?"

His eyes locked on hers, and she thought she saw anger stir in their depths. Her charge obviously rankled him, but he didn't deny it.

She had a certain amount of authority in this relationship, and she intended to exert it. "Well—I suppose I could call you—dear," she said.

He winced. "I'd rather you not call me that, either."

"What?" Her voice rose in surprised aggravation. "'Dear' is perfectly acceptable. Do I have a choice or don't I?" Perrier squirmed in her arms and Trisha realized she was squeezing her, so she put the dog on the ground.

When she met Lassiter's gaze again, she sensed anxiety. He looked away, his nostrils flaring. By the time he faced her again, he was grim, but seemed to have made a decision. "My parents called each other 'dear.' He paused, the muscles of his jaw hardened. "They managed to drench the word in indifference. To me, 'dear' is not a pleasant sound."

She was surprised by his admission and found it telling. Though she'd vowed not to get gooey over this man, her heart went out to him. "Oh—I'm sorry." No wonder he was distant. He'd inherited his lack of emotionalism from cold, unloving parents. She'd never thought of herself as lucky for having only one parent like that. But now she realized she was. How sad it must have been for a boy growing up with two.

Her sip of power suddenly left a bitter aftertaste. "I have no problem with calling you darling, Mr. Dragan," she said, deciding her power wasn't more important than his pain. "It's okay. Really."

He looked as though he regretted his revelation. Being a private person, it had to have been hard. "I appreciate it." He pursed his lips and she sensed he was about to move the subject away from himself. "Satisfy my curiosity," he said, his mask of aloofness dropping firmly into place. "What exactly is a cock's egg?"

She experienced a twinge of distress. She hated not knowing the answer to things, and she didn't know. That was tough to admit, but he'd just told her a hard truth. Surely she had enough gumption to admit she didn't know what a cock's egg was. "I don't recall," she said, "but it's mythic—er—mythological."

He eyed her skeptically. "I thought you were a big reader."

She didn't enjoy being on the defensive. Pulling her chic, military-style coat closer around her, she straightened her shoulders. In a surge of defiance, she said, "Well, I know what a *cock* is!"

Something indefinable sparked in his eyes, looking less like anger than a kindling of respect, an appreciation of her wit. "Is that so?" he asked. "Would your knowledge be mythic—or mythological?" He turned the handle and pushed open one of the doors.

Trisha's lips parted in astonishment. She had no idea how to respond to his flippant feeler into her sexual past. Even if she had, she didn't have time. The next instant, she was swept up in his arms. *"Oh!"* Disoriented, she grabbed his neck and clung on for dear life. "What—"

"Tradition—*sweetheart.*" He stepped across the threshold, his gaze holding hers. His expression was no longer serious, intimidating, but tender, riveting, his sexy grin stunning her into mute reverence. She'd never seen a sight so stimulating and racy and suggestive, and she feared if she ever saw it again, her heart wouldn't survive the pounding.

But what a way to go!

A brilliant flash exploded in her face, blasting her world stark-white. Now she was not only paralyzed, but stone-blind.

"Excellent!" a male voice shouted from a distance. "The perfect homecoming shot!

Lassiter saw them when the door swung open. Two strangers. One held a camera. In that split second, he realized the *Urban Sophisticate* team had arrived early. Sweeping Trisha into his arms had been as much a surprise to him as it had been to her. But once the instinct took hold, he'd acted.

He was amazed by how impulsive he'd become these past few days. He'd never been a spontaneous person, but ever since he'd jotted Herman Hodges' name on that coffee shop napkin, he'd relied less on his logic than his gut.

Before Trisha, he'd never touched women who didn't expect his touch, openly want it. Yet he'd run his finger along the slightly deviant ridge of Trisha's nose as if he'd had a right—not merely an uncontrollable urge.

He'd never moved in on women, crowding them into corners. Not without absolute assurance the woman was willing. And he'd *never* suggested marriage! Never even breathed the word in a woman's presence before. Of course there'd been a sensible and wise rationale, but it was still far and away the most outrageously spontaneous act of his life. And now, without a coherent thought in his head, he'd swept a woman in his arms and whisked her over his threshold. This homecoming scene hadn't been the way he'd planned it at all. But it was done, and apparently done well, since the photographer was unquestionably pleased with what he'd captured on film.

His attention returned to Trisha's face, inches from his own. She blushed well, her color high on cheeks and mouth. It seemed to Lassiter, when she blushed her lips swelled a little—like a sexual prompt from the female animal to the male. A "take me" signal. He experienced an involuntary response that made his blood surge, his gut ache. "We're home, my love," he whispered, only marginally aware as he lowered his lips to hers.

The first contact was cool, but warmed quickly as he moved his mouth over hers, caressing more than kissing. Her lips reminded him of sun-warmed rose petals, the sensation breathtaking. Though her answering kiss was hesitant in her astonishment, she tasted delicious, her lips food for the gods. He experienced a rush of emotion. It billowed and grew until it became a fierce shock wave, reverberating through his body—so charged with electricity, his head snapped up. He felt scorched.

Trisha stared, those come-hither lips slightly parted. Obviously in shock, she regarded him with round, disbelieving eyes. Could he blame her, when he couldn't believe what he'd done, himself? He'd kissed the woman. He hadn't even done that at their wedding. She'd had no inkling, no hint, no warning it was going to happen. No matter that he hadn't either. The point was, she'd never suggested in word or deed that she had any desire to be kissed—at least not by him.

She's your wife, a voice in his head reminded. *Didn't either of you see this as a possibility?* Lassiter realized the likelihood of a kiss should have been discussed. Blast it! Why was hindsight so invariably twenty-twenty when foresight spent so much time stumbling around in the dark?

It was too late for a discussion now. The deed was done. He promised himself to assure her it wouldn't happen again. *Do you have to?* that same bothersome voice cut in. *Tell her it might be necessary to do it a second time—even a third— you idiot! Kissing her was one hell of a trip! You'd like to take that ride again!* He winced, ordering his inner voice to shut up.

Somewhere around the edges of his consciousness he heard a discreet cough. Pulling himself together, Lassiter dragged his attention from Trisha's glittering eyes to notice his butler standing nearby. The white-haired gentleman smiled, as ever, crisp and neat in dark trousers, white dress shirt and jacket, and black bow tie.

"Yes, Marvin?"

"I've made our guests comfortable as you instructed, sir."

"Thank you. And is everything ready for tonight's party?"

Lassiter lowered Trisha to the floor. Damn him if every blasted cell in his body didn't register the long, slow slide of her arms as they slipped from about his neck.

"Yes, sir."

"Thank you, Marvin."

The butler nodded and walked past them to close the door.

Trying to remember his duties as host, Lassiter indicated the man and woman, standing just beyond the stone staircase, its iron railings anchored by a light post. "Sweetheart, these are the magazine people I told you about."

Trisha swayed against him, still disoriented and unsteady on her feet. He placed a supportive arm about her shoulders. "I'm Lassiter Dragan, and this is my bride, Trisha," he said to his guests, then noticed a white fluff ball skitter past them. The dog turned to face her mistress and sat down on the burnt-orange and black runner, her fuzzy face tilted up as she waited to be told what to do.

Lassiter couldn't get used to that four-legged throw pillow being a dog. He thought of dogs as burly beasts that rescued people from collapsed buildings or brought down escaped criminals. Even so, he had to admit, for a wind-up toy Trisha's mutt was well-behaved. "And this is—our dog, Perrier."

The photographer whistled. "Hey, Perrier!"

The dog looked around and got her picture taken. "Pets are great for human interest." Tall and slim, the man with the camera looked to be around Lassiter's age. He wore faded jeans and a black, thermal knit shirt under a short-sleeved, unbuttoned, Hawaiian floral. His long brown hair was tied back in a ponytail. His eyes were a washed-out blue, his smile genuine and toothy. He was probably what women would call classically handsome in the "Greek god" tradition, but for an oversize nose.

The female beside him appeared to be in her early thirties, around Trisha's height and weight. Her face was oval and plain, her brown eyes small, even magnified behind black-framed glasses that were far from trendy, like her gray sweater and corduroy trousers. Her hair was so short it was mannish, the same medium brown color as the photographer's. Though she smiled at them, both her demeanor and her expression told him she was painfully shy.

That surprised Lassiter. He'd assumed a magazine with the international reputation of the *Urban Sophisticate* would hire demonstrative, aggressive reporters. But thinking about it, he supposed retiring types gravitated to careers where they could express themselves in quiet seclusion. Besides, this was a holiday puff piece, not hard-hitting journalism.

He coaxed Trisha toward the couple standing in the wide entry to the great room. When he reached them, he extended a hand, "And you are?"

"Reggie Carter," the photographer said, surprising Lassiter by clasping his hand, since he'd extended it toward the female. "Now this is the rule. You and your pretty bride go about your lives and ignore us. In the best tradition of reality journalism, we're here to capture the Dragans in their natural state." He chuckled, as though at a private joke. "When I say natural, I don't mean—"

"I never thought you did," Lassiter cut in, releasing the man's hand.

"This is Jane Dewey, the best writer at the *Sophisticate*." Reggie patted the woman's shoulder with puppy-dog fervor.

Jane's smile remained shy, but she blushed. Apparently this was a day for female blushes, though Jane's couldn't compete with Trisha's. The reporter nodded a "hello" and put out her hand. "How do you do Mr. Dragan. Mrs. Dragan." She spoke almost too softly to be heard without leaning toward her. "I'm afraid I shall have to bother you from time to time," she went on, barely above a whisper. "Unlike Reggie, I need quotes, family history, holiday chitchat. Five thousand words in all, but I'll try to make it as painless as I can."

"We're delighted to have you." Lassiter squeezed Trisha's shoulder to try to get some kind of response out of her. She seemed dazed. "Aren't we, sweetheart?"

Trisha blinked and smiled, apparently comprehending she needed to react. "Oh—yes. Certainly." She put out a hand. "Jane, so good to meet you." When she released the writer's fingers she took the photographer's. "And Reggie. I'm—delighted."

"We understand this is your honeymoon," Jane said. "And that your romance was a whirlwind thing. I'd love to hear more about it."

Lassiter knew that would come up, considering the story he'd told what's-her-name on the phone. But he didn't want to deal with it right now. Trisha didn't look up to it, either. "Perhaps later. If you'll excuse us, we'd like to—rest after our trip. Then there's the open house tonight." He smiled, indicating his home with a broad wave. "If you'd like a tour, Marvin will be happy to oblige. If you're hungry, there's plenty going on in the kitchen. Somebody can whip you up something. We'll see you around seven.''

''Oh—that's fine,'' Jane said.

''I've already got some great shots.'' Reggie's grin bordered on lascivious.

''Did you?'' Lassiter could just imagine. ''Sweetheart?'' He turned his attention to Trisha. ''Shall we go—rest until the party?''

She glanced his way, looking a little too blank.

''The open house? For Dragan executives?'' He smiled encouragingly.

''Oh—right.'' He could tell she had no idea what he was talking about. Hadn't he mentioned it?

Sliding his arm from about her shoulders, he entwined her fingers with his. ''Well, if you'll excuse us?''

''By all means,'' Jane said in her whispery voice, her blush reappearing. Was she imagining they were going upstairs to while away the afternoon playing wild sex games? His glance slid to Reggie. The photographer's grin was lewd. Damnation! If Jane wasn't thinking ''wild-sex-games,'' Reggie certainly was.

Lassiter smiled, his teeth gritted, and nodded goodbye as he led Trisha by the hand up the curved, limestone staircase. Checking his watch, he calculated there were five hours before they could emerge for his corporate guests and the *Urban Sophisticate* duo. He wondered what in blazes they would do with all those hours, ensconced together in his master bedroom suite?

After only one, brief taste of her lips, Lassiter couldn't think of a more rewarding way to pass those hours than playing sex games with his bride.

Shut up, Dragan! the troublesome voice in his head shouted. *Remember, she may be your legal wife, but you made her a promise about that. She needs a loan, not a lover! And…* the voice jeered, *only days ago, you claimed you didn't need one either.*

CHAPTER SEVEN

TRISHA heard Lassiter's bedroom door close behind them. Slowly, very slowly, she came out of her trance. Had he actually swept her into his arms—then *kissed* her? Her lips felt hot. She reached up, pressing shaky fingers to them. They were. *Hot!* How strange. Running her tongue over her bottom lip, she tasted him and the kiss came rushing back, stealing her breath and setting off Technicolor sparklers behind her eyelids.

She was startled by the fireworks. Had she been standing there with her eyes closed? Trying to banish the memory of his kiss, she opened her eyes and rubbed the back of her hand across her mouth to remove his taste—too stimulating, too delicious. She hadn't seen either performance coming. Lassiter's kiss, right on top of being swept off her feet, was an emotional double-whammy she would have trouble putting behind her.

She'd been in such a state of confusion and disorientation she'd hardly reacted to his kiss. *He must think I'm a terrible cold fish!* She made a pained face. The man could kiss, even without any help. If there were an Olympics event for kissing, he'd have a trophy room brimming with gold medals. *And all you were able to do was go into shock!* Humiliation skewering her chest, she unconsciously placed her hand there. *Why are you humiliated? You don't want the man's love, just his loan! So what if he thinks you kiss like a frozen flounder? You're his smoke screen not his soul mate!*

She could hardly remember what the two magazine people looked like or what she'd said to them. She had stood there, eyes unfocused, her only reality being Lassiter's arm about her. She'd detected his prompts that she snap out of it, when he'd squeezed her shoulders or spoken her name. But the episode blurred in her mind, like a dream. She was still groggy.

"Trisha?"

She heard her name. Lassiter was speaking to her. She turned sluggishly to locate him. "Yes?"

He watched her with an expression she could only describe as concern. "You understand why I kissed you."

She stared, unblinking. "I do?"

He ran a hand over his face, muttering, "You don't." His glance shifted away for a moment and she could hear him exhale. "I'm sorry." He faced her. "I should have discussed the possibility with you. To be honest, it never occurred to me until that moment." He looked perturbed.

He was perturbed? How dare *he* be perturbed! Kissing her never occurred to him until that minute? How flattering! She became aware that their fingers were still entwined. In self-defense, she yanked her hand from his. "Yes—well…" She cleared her throat to bring her voice down an octave. "I suppose I should have expected a certain amount of—of spontaneity."

She took several steps away from him, scanning the large room. Finishes and furnishings exuded comfort and tranquillity. Colors reflected nature, of vernal woods, summer meadows and autumn sunsets. Trisha felt a surprising sense of welcome, considering her mental state, not to mention this was Lassiter Dragan's *bedroom*. Reluctantly focusing on him, she said, "I know we're playing happy newlyweds, but let's try to keep the—er—spontaneity to a minimum."

He slipped his hands into his jeans pockets, looking yummy in a sexy slouch. Why was the man so troublingly seductive, just standing there frowning at her? "That shouldn't be a problem," he said. "I'm not spontaneous by nature."

Hysterical laughter bubbled in her throat, but she stifled it. "You're *not?*" she asked, highly dubious. "You can't tell it by me."

He nodded slowly, as though loathe to admit it. "Lately, I have been—less…" He shifted his gaze to stare past her. She sensed he wasn't looking at fresh snow flurries, visible beyond French doors that lead to a balcony.

He seemed to be looking inward. His long pause didn't do anything for his disposition. When he returned his attention to her he wore a full-fledged scowl. "A dressing room and closet connect to the bathroom," he said, apparently having decided to close the subject of his spontaneity. "I imagine your things have been put away by now. If you'd like to bathe and rest before the party, I'll…" He indicated a rolltop desk beyond a sitting area where Perrier explored. "I have work I can do."

Trisha knew when she was being dismissed, so she nodded. "Sure. I'll go." She had a thought. "I'm surprised you'd have a party on Christmas Eve. That's usually family time."

He raised a dubious eyebrow. "Really? I wouldn't know. My childhood Christmases were spent with servants while my parents went on cruises."

She experienced an unwelcome jab of compassion. "I'm— I'm sorry."

He shook his head as though it was nothing. "To answer your question, it's an open house. People can come early, before family parties, or drop by late, afterward. Those without family nearby can stay all evening. I'm not such a dictator that I'd intentionally sabotage my executive's holiday plans, if that's what you think."

She had to admit, it had crossed her mind. "Well, good. I'm glad to hear it."

"I'm gratified you approve." His tone exhibited more sarcasm than heartfelt sentiment.

She refused to be intimidated. "About this party. What should I wear?"

"It's casual. Wear whatever you please."

That wasn't much help. "Are you going to wear jeans?"

His half smile appeared, but it wasn't the sexy animal it had been when the cameras were clicking. There were no racy sparks, not even a trace of humor. Trisha felt absurdly let down. "Not that casual," he said.

"Right." She started to turn away then had to ask, "What exactly are we going to tell these people—I mean they work for you. Don't you feel—uncomfortable about presenting me as your—soul mate?''

He pondered her question, his features neither delighted nor guilt-ridden. ''Uncomfortable? Yes, a little.''

''But not so uncomfortable that millions of dollars worth of advertising can't fix?'' she suggested.

He watched her for a moment with unreadable eyes. ''What helps me helps Dragan Ventures,'' he said. ''And what helps Dragan Ventures helps the people I employ.''

He didn't sound defensive, or offended, just matter-of-fact. ''And what helps me, helps you,'' he reminded. ''You're not getting cold feet are you?''

She crossed her arms, trying not to be intimidated by his steely stare. ''Don't worry. I need that loan.''

''True,'' he said. ''To answer your question, the story we tell is exactly as it happened, except when it comes to the loan. We say it was love at first sight in the coffee shop—a whirlwind courtship and the Las Vegas wedding. Got it?''

She supposed if he had so few qualms about fooling people he saw every day, some of them his close confidants, she could go along. After all, they were actually married. They just weren't in love. Besides, she would never see them again after the new year.

Including her holiday husband.

She felt a stab of regret, but tried to ignore it. Shrugging, she nodded. ''I've got it, Mr. Dragan.''

He watched her. She felt vulnerable and out of her league. Too often she had no idea what went on in his mind. ''It would be better if you called me 'darling' while you're in my home. I wouldn't want a stray 'Mr. Dragan' to slip out when we're not alone.''

She felt a contrary spasm of desire squeeze her chest. She'd thought calling him ''darling'' would be too easy. But it wasn't. Not like this. She looked away, took a deep breath, but felt no calmer. ''Whatever you say—*darling*.'' Their glances clashed, his cool gaze giving her no hope her endearment affected him even slightly.

* * *

The party was in full swing. She and Lassiter spent the first hour in the foyer, greeting guests as they arrived. Clearly Lassiter was up to their newlywed plot. If she hadn't know better, she would have thought he was her affectionate bridegroom. His closeness, his touches, his endearing glances, were difficult to deal with, especially since she had to pretend to be his loving bride while battling a foolish attraction to him.

After the first rush of guests dwindled to the occasional new arrival, Lassiter suggested they mix and mingle. His beautiful mansion was large, so she took advantage of that. If she managed to become separated from him, she quickly lost herself in the crowd. Several times she'd escaped to get breathing space and allow her heart rate to slow to normal. Nodding at smiling guests, she kept on the move, nibbling from hors d'oeuvres trays and taking in the sights like a hick tourist in a fancy hotel.

The rooms of Lassiter Dragan's home stretched out like vines, open and contemporary, yet with a traditional feel. Everywhere she turned she saw rustic beauty. So far she'd counted three massive hearths of recycled brick and limestone; blazing wood fires scented the air and warmed rooms decorated with a tasteful Mediterranean flair.

Wandering around among Dragan employees, with no idea where she was, she allowed herself to forget the ploy for long moments at a time, noticing tons of rich detail and old-world character, like textured plaster walls and exposed antique heart-pine beams. If she hadn't heard Lassiter, himself, mention the house was a mere decade old, she wouldn't have believed it. Walls, floors and ceilings gave the impression of authentic old surfaces, lovingly restored.

She caught her reflection in one of the tall windows and stared, still unaccustomed to seeing herself in such upscale fashions. She'd never had clothes like the red, off-the-shoulder sweater and matching stretch gabardine trousers. Cut low, they left a peek-a-boo strip of skin exposed beneath the body-hugging top. It seemed silly in wintertime to have bare skin peeping out of your clothes, but Lassiter had only told her to buy them, not understand them.

Her Christmas wreath pin sparkled like it was made of real jewels instead of cheap glass. She touched it fondly. "Merry Christmas, Mama," she whispered. This was her first Christmas without her mother. Sadness rushed in quickly and she had to turn away, look at something else, think of something else. This was no time to burst into tears. She decided it was good that she was here, in such a foreign setting. It would help keep her mind off...

She looked around frantically, wanting to redirect her thoughts. *Concentrate on the house,* she told herself. It was a nice house, she decided, then shook her head at the enormity of her understatement. It was a magnificent mansion, a feast for the eye. Yet, somehow it managed to seem cozy and intimate.

Maybe it was the low lighting. Or the flicker of strategically placed candles. Or the pleasant fires blazing in the hearths. Whatever it was that made the place homey rather than museum-like, discriminating yet unpretentious, she was thankful. It was hard enough being the blushing bride of such a powerful, intimidating man. She couldn't cope if the trappings were equally intimidating.

She glanced at the floor, admiring a sumptuous Oriental rug, in muted hues of terra-cotta and moss green. She loved Oriental rugs, but knew she would never be able to afford a real, handmade masterpiece like the one she stood on. She felt wicked wearing shoes. It was like tromping on a Van Gogh.

She had an awful urge to kick off her chunky-soled loafers. Awful and overwhelming. The notion was preposterous, considering where she was and who she was supposed to be. Chewing her lower lip with uncertainty, she looked around. Would anybody notice with the lights so low?

Making a quick decision she sat down on a sofa in a conversation area before a crackling hearth. Quickly slipping off her loafers and socks she stuck them underneath the couch. Relaxing, she lolled her head on the back cushion and closed her eyes. Sliding her bare feet back and forth, back and forth, she luxuriated in the tingling caress of the rug's texture. Calm for the first time since she'd walked into the Dragan building a lifetime ago, she sighed. "Oh, Trisha," she murmured, "You have an unnatural passion for Oriental rugs."

"Then you should be ashamed of yourself."

She recognized Lassiter's deep voice, very close, and snapped open her eyes. The first sight she saw was his face above hers, but upside-down. He stood behind the sofa, leaning down, resting his hands on either side of her head. "You're hard to keep track of, sweetheart." His grin was slightly askew, teeth flashing. Even topsy-turvy, the erotic effect was immediate and intoxicating. *Heavens above!* How that man could grin—when it paid him to.

She jerked forward and stood, twisting to face him. "I— I'm sorry. I was just..."

"Being unnaturally passionate with my rug, I know." He walked around the sofa and held out a hand, looking scrumptious in slim, black trousers and V-neck sweater. There were no phony detractions, nothing about his attire to remove the eye or the mind from how cunningly nature had constructed him. Merely accepting his hand could be dangerous. She hesitated. "Several couples have just come in who want to meet you," he said. "People are curious."

"I bet," she said. He laced his fingers with hers, and she experienced a lightning-quick surge of excitement. *Exactly* the feeling she'd been trying to avoid by making herself scarce. "Oh—my shoes and socks." She started to dive for them, but his hold on her hand stopped her.

"Leave them." His smile hadn't changed, but Trisha saw an unfamiliar glint in his eyes, as though he found her eccentricity over Oriental rugs engaging. "Indulge your passion. The house is full of rugs."

She looked at him quizzically, then found herself smiling, astounded that his tiniest show of approval held such power. It frightened her, but just now, looking into his eyes, the power was too strong to fight. "You don't think it's too—twisted?"

"It's very twisted." He coaxed her in the direction of what she believed was the great room. "I'm shocked."

She glanced at his profile and realized he was teasing. Taking off one's shoes and socks wasn't exactly listed in the dictionary under "kinky." "I get it. You think readers who like to go without shoes will see my bare feet and clamor to be your clients."

He glanced her way, scanned her all the way to her bare toes, then up to her face. He flashed another of those high-wattage grins. "Or I might just think you have cute feet."

As he pulled her along, she stared, dumbfounded. "You think I have cute feet?"

He met her gaze. "You have beautiful feet. Hasn't anyone ever told you that?"

"Oh—sure," she said. "All the time. In the summer when I'm wearing sandals, people come up to me just to admire my feet. Tourists take pictures."

Sliding his arm about her shoulders, he displayed another heart-stopping grin. "Sweetheart, this is Herman Hodges, my right-hand man." The abrupt change in subject jarred her but she managed a nod. She hadn't noticed Mr. Hodges. Hadn't even realized she'd been maneuvered into a cluster of people.

Lassiter's hand slid up to cup her bare shoulder, his fingers grazing her collarbone. The sensation sent a warm tingle coursing through her, and she found it harder than it should be to follow the mundane niceties.

Did he really think she had cute feet or had he been flattering her, wangling smiles from her to fool the crowd? Had Reggie been snapping pictures all along, as he was now? She had no idea, she'd been so lost in Lassiter's eyes. *Trisha, it does not matter if you were being manipulated for photo opportunities or if your provisional husband gives a fig about your feet! Focus! Say something to Mr. Hodges!*

She put out her hand. "It's so nice to—meet you, Mr. Hodges. Merry Christmas."

The older man's smile was pained. She could tell by his concerned expression that he, alone among Lassiter's guests, had grave doubts about their "love at first sight" story.

They shook hands. "A pleasure—Mrs. Dragan," Hodges said.

"Oh, call me Trisha, please." She wished she had more control over her blushes. Her face blazed, but she struggled to remain poised. She might be Lassiter's lawful bride, but this scheme was still one huge lie as far as her conscience was concerned.

"I'd like you to meet my wife, Cecilia," Herm Hodges went on.

Trisha exchanged small talk with Herm and his wife before being introduced to another vice president and his date. She tried desperately to keep all the names straight, but after meeting so many couples, she feared it was a losing battle.

The rangy blond, vice president she'd just met was Greg—something—in a loud Christmas sweater. He looked more like a Nordic ski instructor than a venture capitalist. After some polite chitchat, he finally said what everybody had obviously been thinking. "We're all shell shocked by Gent's sudden marriage."

Trisha didn't blame them, but she stuck to the script, improvising, "Lassit—that is—*my darling* swept me off my feet. He's *so* impulsive!"

Greg choked on an hors d'oeuvre. Everyone within earshot went stock-still and stared, some openmouthed. Apparently Lassiter's statement about himself had been true. He was definitely *not* known for his impulsiveness.

He cleared his throat and Trisha suspected she was being reprimanded. What did he expect her to say? There weren't many scenarios open to them beside impulsiveness and insanity. Considering everything, insanity might be closer to the truth.

CHAPTER EIGHT

AT MIDNIGHT the last of Lassiter's guests went home. During the whole evening Trisha had hardly seen Jane, the magazine journalist. When she had, the shy woman had been like a ghost, standing in corners, observing. Not long after ten o'clock, Jane retired to her bedroom.

Reggie was Jane's exact opposite. Outgoing and gregarious, he hung on until the last, taking pictures, laughing and joking, having fun. While the kitchen staff cleared away the food, he chased them down heaping snacks on a plate. With his treasure trove of delicacies, he settled in front of the big-screen TV in the den, bidding the newlyweds a leering "sweet dreams."

Lassiter and Trisha went upstairs, hand in hand, for show. Once inside Lassiter's bedroom, Trisha noticed the flicker of flames. "Oh, somebody started a fire in here," she said, delighted.

"We're lucky it's in the fireplace."

She didn't expect a joke, and turned toward Lassiter. Against her will, she smiled. "Cute." Even his nonchalant touch was too stimulating, so she disengaged her fingers from his and walked to the hearth. "The party was more fun than I expected," she said, thinking aloud more than commenting. "All those powerful people turned out to be—well, plain, normal people." She smiled down at Perrier who came up wagging her stubby tail. "I even met a few who are as nutty about animals as I am."

"You looked like you were having a good time."

She glanced his way. He lounged against the bedroom door in an elegant slouch, hands in his pockets and legs crossed at the ankles. With his raven-dark hair, brilliant eyes and clad all in black, he could have been the cover model for *Spellbinder* magazine, had there been such a thing.

She realized she was staring and tried to get back on track. What had he said? Something about her having a good time? Yes, that was it. "Um—I really did. They were nice people."

Keyed up, but feeling an odd weakness in her knees, she broke eye contact and plopped down on the room-size Oriental rug. The fire felt good and she basked in its warmth. So many years ago, after her father walked out, she and her mom had been forced to move to a cheap apartment, never again living where there was a fireplace. She hadn't realized how much she'd missed a real wood fire until Lassiter reintroduced them into her life. Deciding he wouldn't care one way or the other, she lowered herself to her back and closed her eyes. The wood smelled nice. She stretched on the rug like a contented cat, inhaling the hickory scent deep into her lungs.

"Indulging your unnatural passion for rugs again?"

She lolled her head in the direction of his voice and opened her eyes. "Um hum." He'd moved closer, and towered above her, a mountain of male animal. He watched her almost as though she were a foreign species, not with distaste or disdain, but with curiosity.

"Don't you ever lie on a rug in front of a fire?" she asked.

He cocked his head, eyeing her with a wry expression. "Not by myself, no."

Oh! She could almost hear him add, *"And not with my clothes on."* The visions that sprang into her mind made her blush. *You ran right into that one, Trisha!*

Clearing her throat, she moved her attention to the fire, determined to change the subject. "After my father left us, Mom and I lived in a basement apartment. For ten years our floors were bare concrete." The words "cold, harsh and damp" came to her mind, but she preferred to remember her mother's buoyant spirit and how she made the best of their situation. "We painted the floors with bright flowers and designs." Of course, painting the concrete didn't alleviate the harshness or the coldness or the dampness, but simply thinking about those brightly painted floors, being reminded of her mother's cheerful optimism, made her smile.

"Didn't your mother get alimony and child support?"

She shook her head. "Mother didn't want anything from dad and neither did I. Not even his name. August is my mother's maiden name." She clutched her hands together, amazed that even the recollection of that sad time in her life could still upset her so much. "Though Mom never said so, I think she knew he wouldn't hand over any of his precious money, so refusing it allowed her to believe he *might* have, if he'd been asked to. I think Mom needed to believe he wasn't as heartless as—well, that he wasn't heartless."

When Lassiter didn't respond, she felt the need to fill the silence. "Mother cleaned houses for a living. I went with her on weekends. The place she cleaned on Saturdays had beautiful rugs—like yours. The lady who lived there was an invalid. Sometimes we'd talk, and she'd tell me about her paintings, her porcelains and her Oriental rugs."

Trisha couldn't help turning to gauge his expression. He watched her, brows knit. Restless under his scrutiny, she dragged her hands through the rug's nap until her arms were stretched out to her sides. The move tickled her palms. "You never gave a thought to the work and talent that goes into creating these marvelous things, did you?"

He half grinned and shook his head. "No. But from now on, I won't look at them in the same way." He held out a hand. "You don't intend to sleep there, do you?"

She closed her eyes. Though it had been a long, stressful day, she was too keyed up to sleep. She hoped lying before the fire might help her grow drowsy, as it had when she was little. "Why not? It's warm and cozy."

"It won't be once the fire dies down."

"I'll turn on the gas."

"Is this your way of saying you have no plans to sleep with me?"

His shocking query exploded any hope of tranquil slumber before the fire. Instantly alert she scrambled to sit up. "I beg your pardon?" She watched him with a hammering heart. Why must he be so handsome? Why must the flickering firelight enhance his cheekbones, his silvery eyes and strong square chin? "Of—of course, I have no plans to sleep with you," she said. "I didn't think it needed discussing." She pointed toward the conversation area. A forest-green couch and two plaid wing chairs separated his king size sleigh-styled bed and his rolltop desk. "I thought I'd sleep—"

"Wrong," he interrupted, grasping her raised hand. "You'll take the bed. I'll take the couch, and Perrier can sleep on the rug." He pulled her to her feet. "No debates."

"But it's your—"

"Not while you're here." He indicated the bathroom. "I suggest you get ready for bed. I told Reggie and Jane we'd meet them for breakfast at eight."

"Oh?"

He nodded, his expression serious, a man not to be argued with. "Christmas morning with the Dragans. We'll have a traditional breakfast and then open our gifts."

Trisha was confused. "What traditional breakfast? What gifts?"

He shrugged. "I'm not sure what the breakfast will be, since I left that up to cook. My secretary, Cindy, handled the gifts for me over the weekend, along with getting a tree."

Trisha was stunned. "You—you mean you didn't already have that beautiful tree up and decorated?" The blue spruce in Lassiter's great room was at least fifteen feet tall, and trimmed with spectacular ornaments. Some looked like family heirlooms.

"No. Right after my Christmas Eve open house, I fly to my condo in Vail, meet friends and ski until New Year's Day."

"Oh?" Why did she feel a prick of jealousy? Her question about what gifts he'd been referring to flew right out of her head with the bombshell about Vail and skiing with friends. What *friends?* Did that translate into couples? And did Lassiter mean he met a woman friend there and they... *Don't be an idiot, Trisha! Naturally, he did! And they did! What era are you living in, Puritan, America?* "You were going this year?" she asked.

He nodded. "I go every year."

She was surprised. "Don't you have family you spend the holidays with?"

"Not since my parents died."

She experienced a stab of compassion. "Oh, I'm so sorry— how—"

"Car crash when I was twenty-five." She noticed a slight narrowing of his eyes and a side-to-side motion of his jaw, as though the subject distressed him.

"I thought you said you'd never known great loss," she said. "Losing your parents suddenly and so tragically—"

"Death is part of life," he cut in.

"So is grieving," she countered. "It's not a sin."

"They've been gone a long time, Miss August," he said. "Shall we change the subject?"

Trisha had known he was a private person, but she hadn't realized he'd wrapped his emotions in a little ball and stuffed them in a mental freezer. How sad. "Sure, okay." Subject change. His comment about Christmas at the Vail condo with *friends* still nagged at her. Though she didn't care to know details, she found it the only topic that came to mind. "So— since you aren't going to your condo this year, what will happen with your—friends?"

"My caretaker has the key, so I'm sure they'll enjoy my condo along with the thirty new inches of powder that accumulated over the weekend."

He must be terribly disappointed! Trisha felt sick to her stomach. "Oh—I'm sorry…"

"Why?" he asked. "The magazine article was my decision. You didn't spoil my vacation."

She avoided looking at him. "But you probably invited a— a girlfriend…" She couldn't finish the sentence, though there was no need. It didn't take a rocket scientist to follow her "girlfriend" theory through to its natural conclusion.

He didn't say anything, and she couldn't look at him. He may have said she didn't spoil his vacation, but if she looked in his eyes she was positive she would see the awful truth— his displeasure over being deprived of exhilarating days of skiing and nights of holiday sex. Suddenly she felt exhausted. "Yes—well…" She headed toward the bathroom.

"What did I spoil for you?" he asked.

Confused, she halted, shifted to look back. "What?"

"You had holiday plans," he said. "Anyone who gets so passionate about Oriental rugs and fires in the hearth has to have holiday plans."

She was surprised he'd asked. She'd doubted he ever would, believing his own interests were all that mattered to him. That trait had been one of her father's most disagreeable failings.

"Do you really care?" she asked.

He watched her, his expression unreadable. After a moment, he said, "Of course." Annoyance edged his tone. "If I didn't, I wouldn't ask."

He actually seemed bothered by her assumption that he didn't care. Or was it merely that he was so powerful he expected answers to his questions, and any evasions or disputes irritated him?

"All right, all right." She touched her mother's wreath pin, stroked it, calming herself. "When Mom was alive, we served meals to the homeless on Christmas day." She winced at the horrible pain that came with the reminder of her mother's passing. "After Mom remarried, my stepdad joined us. Mother passed away last March. Complications from surgery." Her voice broke and she swallowed to regain her poise. "So my stepdad went to Albuquerque to see his daughter and grand-kids this Christmas." She stared at the flames wrapping around the aromatic, hickory logs. "My landlady knew I was alone, so she invited me to come to her family's celebration, but…"

"I'm sorry."

She flicked her gaze to his. "It's no big deal, I didn't…"

"I meant about your mother."

His insincerity outraged her. "Oh, *please*. I know your philosophy."

"Trisha," he said. "No matter what you think, I'm not completely devoid of humanity. You just lost your mother. Of course, I'm sorry. You two were very close, weren't you?"

That diplomatic speech held a ring of truth that magically melted away Trisha's anger. Her logical side reminded her that he was a master at diplomacy. Look at his nickname. *Gent!*

The Gentleman Dragon. Diplomacy was just a pretty word for one-upmanship, jockeying for position. Good grief! She was married to the man because of his smooth, persuasive gift of the gab. Even so, she chose to believe him, with no idea why.

"Mom was wonderful." Trisha blinked back tears. "I was eighteen when she married Gerard, a sweet man, a widower. He drove a delivery truck and he liked to fish. Vacations, he and Mom camped and fished. They lived simple but full lives. Mom was happy with Gerard and I was happy for her."

She smiled wanly. "Gerard's house was tiny, so when they got married I naturally got a place of my own." She shifted her attention back to the fire. "As soon as I could afford it, I bought a rug." She stared at the flames, but looked inward. "It's a cheap imitation, but I love it," she said with a melancholy smile. "I couldn't bear to walk on it, so I hung it on the wall." She laughed but the memory was more poignant than amusing. "Mom always thought that was so funny." Her heart hurt the way it always did when she recalled happier times with her mother, and how terribly she missed her.

Running a hand through her hair, she attempted to improve her mood. Her mother would have been the last person in the world to want her to be sad over the holidays. "I think—I'll get ready for bed." She kept her eyes averted to hide a telltale sheen of sadness. "Good night—Mr.—er—darling."

"Good night." He watched her walk barefoot across the rug, so striking in the red, body-hugging trousers and off-the-shoulder tease of a sweater. Her hair was in no particular style. It fell in loose, free waves, doing its own flirty thing, haloing her face in a golden aura. She had the most impudent *hair* he'd ever come across. It fairly dared him to run his fingers through it. During the party he'd had to use every ounce of self-control to keep his hands out of the stuff.

He'd never thought of himself as the knuckle-dragging sort, but watching her walk away with what he could only describe as a come-hither sway—which he knew was *not* her intention—he was reminded of the caveman cliché about keeping a woman barefoot and pregnant. Intellectually, he knew such thinking was Neanderthal nonsense, but at this moment, the idea appealed to him more than he liked to admit.

Whoa! Dragan! Get a grip! So the woman isn't wearing shoes! You've seen barefooted women before. Hell, you've seen bare-everything women before. Swaying hips, tempting hair and naked feet shouldn't make you go all Homo erectus! He winced. What kind of primitive-man-Freudian-slip was that?

When Trisha closed the bathroom door behind her, Lassiter drew his first full breath since she'd begun to walk away. He noticed movement and eyed the white fur ball pitter-patting to face him, practically wagging itself in two. He frowned. "Mutt, you'd better be worth at least a million in free advertising." He ground his teeth. "As for your owner in there, she'd better—" He cut himself off, scowled into the fire. "First, she needs to—"

He bit off a curse, not sure what he was angry about or why he felt the need to vent in a grumbled soliloquy to a dumb animal. "Free advertising or no free advertising, she should quit—*damnation!*" Quit what? What was she doing that was so all-fired wrong?

It wasn't like him to stumble around mentally. Why in Hades couldn't he get one simple thought stated? What exactly was that one simple thought he wanted to state? What was it about the woman that plagued him, agitated him, made him babble incoherently—and to a dog, yet?

He glared at the mutt, then into the fire, then back at the mutt. *She needs a loan, not a lover,* an internal voice reminded. "I know that!" he groused, tired of hearing that same, annoying harangue in his head a hundred times a day. Shoving both hands through his hair, he growled, "Shut up, Dragan, and not one blasted word about the woman being your *wife,* either. She's not *that* kind of a wife! Go to bed!"

Their sleeping arrangements were worrisome, but by the time Trisha peeped out of the bathroom, Lassiter had made himself a bed on the couch. He looked uncomfortable, his long legs projecting out over the arm. She watched him nervously. He didn't move. With an arm thrown over his eyes, he appeared to be asleep. She didn't know what he might be wearing, since a sheet covered him from chest to calf. The uncovered areas were bare, so that troubled her.

When she thought about it logically, she knew he must be wearing something. After all...she wasn't sure how to finish that sentence. After all, a business arrangement might mean she was on her own in the modesty department. If he wanted to sleep in the nude on his own sofa, it didn't affect her loan. She could only pray that he hadn't figured it like that.

Finally, after several long, courage-building breaths, she dashed to the big bed, scrambled beneath the covers and turned away from him. Watching him wouldn't help her get to sleep.

An hour later, she faced the fact that turning her back didn't help. Another hour dragged by, then another, still she couldn't sleep. The bed was comfortable but the room unfamiliar. The house made strange noises and, of course, the most troubling and pervasive reason she couldn't sleep was—*Lassiter Dragan slept nearby.*

Making a bad situation worse, Perrier was accustomed to sleeping on the bed with her, so after resisting her dog's whining pleas until three o'clock in the morning, Trisha gave in and lifted her pet up to join her, deciding she would deal with Mr. Dragan's wrath when the time came or get no sleep at all.

By dawn, she gave up trying to sleep and slipped quietly out of bed. She'd dressed in jeans and a flannel shirt and had almost finished tying her second boot before Lassiter stirred. Sensing he was waking, she fumbled with the leather laces, dropped them, and had to start again. When she heard him sit up, she struggled not to look at him.

"Good morning," he said, sounding grumpy.

From the place on the rug where she'd settled to pull on her boots, she peeked in his direction. "Good morning." To her dismay, she couldn't drag her gaze away. He hunched there, resting forearms on thighs. The sheet covered his lap and not much else. All that bare skin looked taut and tempting in the rosy glow of dawn. He peered at his wristwatch. "It's six.'' His frown grew less grumpy and more puzzled. ''What are you doing?''

She indicated Perrier. ''I have to take her out.''

He nodded in understanding and ran a hand over his face. ''Sleep well?''

''Beautifully,'' she lied. ''And you?'' She made a face. That was a stupid question. How well could he have slept on that cramped excuse for a bed?

''Do you know about fakirs who sleep on beds of nails?'' he asked.

She nodded.

''I would kill for one of those beds.''

Trying to squelch an urge to smile, she lowered her head and finished tying her boot. He shouldn't make jokes if he wanted her sympathy to appear genuine. When she managed to quell the urge to smile, she looked up. ''I'm sorry.''

He waved it off. ''One of the servants can take the dog out. You don't need to get dressed in jeans and boots, just for that.''

''It's okay. I'll be wearing these today, anyway.'' She bit her lip. He'd cut her off last night when she'd been about to tell him her plans. She hoped he would take the news like the gentleman dragon he was alleged to be.

His frown returned. How could he look groggy and cuddly and sexy all at the same time? ''Jeans and boots on Christmas day? Don't you think that's too casual for what we have planned?''

''We?'' she asked, her tone meaningful. ''You mean what *you* have planned.'' She shook her head, dreading what the next few moments would bring. But she was determined. There were no ifs, ands or buts about what she intended to do today. ''I'm sorry, Lassiter. I have to go.''

''What do you mean you have to go?'' Anger touched his features. ''Don't tell me you've decided not to go through with our deal.''

She couldn't believe he would jump to that conclusion. ''Of course not. I honor my agreements—no matter how money-grubbing.'' She cursed herself. *That's right, Trisha, make him mad. That'll help!* Obviously she hadn't had enough sleep—plus the sight of so much stimulating, male skin was getting on her nerves.

Trying for calm, she stood up and leaned against the curved footboard of his bed. "What I mean is, what *we* have planned and what *I* have planned are two entirely different days." She shrugged, sheepish. "I told you on Christmas Mom and I helped feed the homeless. We always went to The Sister of Celestial Love shelter to serve Christmas dinner. It's the way we celebrated the holiday, and just because she's—gone, well, I have no intention of quitting." She indicated his expensively appointed bedroom. "All this only makes the difference between the haves and the have-nots more glaring, and my need to help more undeniable."

He sat up straight, his hands on his knees. Trisha was sorry he did, since it showed off his broad chest and washboard belly to better advantage. "Don't be foolish," he said, his expression hard.

She felt a rush of disappointment. Why? She knew what he was like. Her father would have said the same thing. "It's not foolish to want to help others, Lassiter."

"Have you forgotten the magazine article?" he asked. "My kitchen staff are preparing a huge meal."

"And I'm sure it will be delicious." Trisha plucked Perrier off the floor. "As for the article, you'll look like Father Christmas, donating that wonderful meal to the shelter." Hurrying out the door, she peeked at him. He couldn't have looked more shocked if she'd told him she planned to set his house on fire.

CHAPTER NINE

LASSITER could not believe he was spending Christmas day in a neglected, inner city residential neighborhood. The building the Celestial Sisters homeless shelter occupied was an abandoned elementary school, built in the early nineteen fifties. The wood floors were worn but clean, the institutional walls enlivened by murals of smiling, dancing children in sunny meadows, brimming with flowers—clearly more an effort to lift spirits than to exhibit artistic genius.

The "gymtorium" served as the heart of the facility. It was there that residents slept in bunk beds in a barracks-like setting. Women and children were quartered on the stage behind a cloth barricade, while men bedded down on the main level. Lodgers had access to bathrooms and showers, as well as the school's cafeteria, where *his* Christmas dinner had been parceled out to vagabond diners.

He hadn't had a bite of his favorite appetizer, a savory lobster cheesecake, sliced and served with a Creole-spiced tomato-tarragon coulis. It disappeared as briskly as his visions of the ideal magazine shoot he'd planned for today, along with the succulent roasted turkey that nobody on earth could prepare as well as his chef, André. Not to mention the delicious wilted spinach salad with its warm andouille sausage dressing. To top off his Christmas feast, he'd requested André's ambrosial banana cream pie. At least, he'd seen a few pieces of it being enthusiastically consumed—from a distance—as hordes of homeless strangers filled their bellies with his food, along with donated dishes from local churches, businesses and other individuals.

Lassiter's job had been to hand out meal tickets and paper cups of steaming coffee to those who had waited in line for hours outside in subfreezing cold. He'd never realized that

103

some people who came to homeless shelters to eat actually had homes, but couldn't stretch their budgets all the way to the end of the month to buy food. He'd also been surprised by how many of those waiting in line for a seat and a meal were little kids. Some hadn't even had gloves. Seeing those chapped, red, shivery little fingers, he wished he had more than hot coffee to hand out.

For years, when he'd made donations to the United Way, he'd never thought about the human element of homelessness, that there were actual children out there who didn't have adequate food, shelter or clothing. "A little self-absorbed are we, Dragan?" he muttered.

"Having fun?"

The din of voices from the packed cafeteria tables, along with the constant clank of silverware, had masked Trisha's approach. He turned away from the door to face her. No new arrivals had come in since six-thirty, fifteen minutes ago, so he had a feeling his ticket taking duties might be drawing to a close. "I wouldn't say it's been rip-roaring hilarious, but I've got no complaints." He was startled to realize he really didn't.

She smiled at him, and he noticed again how naturally pretty she was, even with the little crook in her nose. "I hope you'll still feel that way in a minute," she said.

He eyed her suspiciously. "Why? What new, Christmas charity chicanery have you got percolating in your scary brain? Are we giving away my house?"

She laughed, the sound sliding pleasantly across his consciousness. "Not yet." Taking his hand, she towed him past the rows of long cafeteria tables teaming with humanity's downtrodden. "We need your vast, corporate leadership qualities to wrest an accumulation of sustenance utensils from a besmirched state to immaculateness."

The clamor of voices and the clangor of silverware against pottery was noisy, but not so noisy that he couldn't decipher her meaning. "You want me to wash dishes?" He was surprised that he wasn't surprised by her presumptuousness.

She'd already given away his Christmas dinner, why shouldn't she believe she could get his hands into dishwater?

Her smile broadened and her eyebrows rose, as though impressed by his code-cracking ability. "Wow, I thought I'd get you closer to the kitchen before you figured it out."

He frowned at her. "Wasn't sacrificing my banana cream pie enough abuse for one Christmas?"

"It can't be helped. Two of the kitchen volunteers had to leave," she said. "By the way, the pie was delicious."

He stared at her with misgiving. "You got a piece?"

She nodded. "Petunia forced it on me."

"Oh she did, did she?" Lassiter pictured the two so-called Celestial Sisters who ran the place. Not the saintly ideal he'd envisioned, they wore camouflage army fatigues and were blunt and loud. Lassiter's name was well-known in Kansas City, and he was accustomed to a show of recognition, some deference, even occasional fawning from those who met him. None of that happened when Peg Ray and Petunia Cook were introduced to him.

Clearly not into bowing and scraping, the women did not thank him profusely for his marvelous donation. When he'd stretched out a hand in greeting, Peg slapped him on the back with enough force to knock him forward a step, while Petunia bellowed, "Thanks for the grub, bub!" and put him to work handing out tickets and coffee. "Nobody forced my banana cream pie on me," he groused, though it was more mocking than real. After all, André could always make another banana cream pie. "So far today I've had one broken oatmeal cookie and all the hot coffee I could give away."

"And look at how majestically you've borne up under all that hardship," she teased. "I'm in awe."

"Sure you are." Lassiter allowed her to tug him along, wondering what it was that kept him from breaking free of her light hold on his hand? What kept him from sternly explaining that Lassiter Dragan had never washed a dish in his life, and didn't plan to start now? Could it possibly be the sight of her smile?

Ever since they'd arrived, he'd found himself seeking her

out with his eyes. He watched her laugh and joke with Reggie whenever their paths crossed. The photographer was a free-spirited, friendly sort, taking pictures all over the shelter, while discreetly obscuring faces of the homeless to safeguard their privacy.

Somewhere around midafternoon, the fact that Trisha laughed openly and readily with the photographer had started to bother him. She was freer and friendlier with a near stranger than she was with the man she was supposed to be married to. Oh, sure, she smiled, but most of the smiles had been part of the just-married act, like last night at the party.

So when she'd smiled just now, a real smile, as though she found him worthy of her approval, simply standing around a homeless shelter all day, it affected him so strongly the idea of washing dishes became almost acceptable. It was a weird thing to discover about a woman's smile—that it could beguile him into a rundown kitchen and seduce him into rolling up his sleeves to toil like a day laborer. He shook his head at his lamblike compliance, choosing not to analyze it, which was also weird, since he was an analyzer by nature.

Besides Trisha's siren smile, he had to give her credit for another appealing attribute—knowing how to peddle character, even if she wasn't aware that was what she was doing. This open-handed holiday outing would be heart-tugging puffery for the article.

"Daddy?"

Lassiter felt a tug and looked down to see a big-eyed little boy clutching the bottom ribbing of his turtleneck sweater. The child was barely tall enough to reach up that far, but with his arms stretched over his head, he held wads of navy cashmere in both fists as though his life depended on not letting go. "Daddy?" he repeated, his face pinched and woebegone.

Lassiter guessed the boy was about four years old, but considering his lack of knowledge about children, he could have been way off. The boy's hair was dark and curly, his eyes a deep brown. He wore a faded sweatshirt with some cartoon superhero on the front, brown corduroy britches that had seen better days, and scuffed boots, wet from melted snow.

Lassiter didn't know what to do or say. Since the child's desperate hold on his sweater had forced him to stop, Trisha stopped, too. He registered the fact that she released his hand. A second later, she knelt beside the child. "Hello," she said. "What's your name?"

The child shifted his unhappy expression from Lassiter to Trisha. "Pedro Rodriguez." He looked back up at Lassiter. "Daddy?"

Lassiter glanced at Trisha for guidance. What did one do when a tiny Pedro Rodriguez grabbed you and called you "daddy"?

Trisha smiled wanly as if to say "I'll see what I can do," and returned her attention to the boy. "Pedro, does Mr. Dragan look like your daddy?"

The child nodded, his lower lip trembling. He didn't loosen his hold on Lassiter's sweater. "I want my daddy."

A woman sitting at the table turned, seeming to notice the boy was no longer seated beside her. "Pedro, what are you doing?"

The child continued to focus on Lassiter with those big eyes, now brimming with tears. "I want my daddy."

"Oh, dear," the woman said, her expression troubled and apologetic. She looked to be about twenty, skinny to the point of bony, a pretty face, sad blue eyes and short, dishwater blond hair. She lifted her gaze to Lassiter. "Pedro, let go of the nice man. He's not—" She swallowed, as though trying to get herself under control. "His father passed away three weeks ago." She blinked as though fighting tears. "Pul—uh—pulmonary embolism. You look—a little—like..." She bit her lip. "Juan had dark hair like you, but he wasn't as tall. I guess to a four-year-old..." She shook her head, unable to go on. Reaching out, she untangled her son's fingers from Lassiter's sweater. "Pedro, this isn't Daddy. Remember what we talked about? Daddy's gone to heaven."

Lassiter experienced a twinge of pity. Poor kid. He was not much more than a baby but he'd lost his dad, which obviously left him and his young mother in financial straits, since they were eating Christmas dinner in a homeless shelter. Growing up, Lassiter had thought having cold parents was grim. *Hell!* He could take a few lessons from little Pedro on the meaning of grim.

He found himself kneeling. "Hey, Pedro," he said with a smile, "My name's Lassiter." It pained him to watch a tear dangle from the child's lower lashes, then slide down his cheek, still rosy from waiting outside in the cold. "Did Santa Claus come to visit you today?"

He heard a sharp gasp and flicked his gaze to the child's mother. The young widow shook her head sharply, her expression miserable. "Uh—we—just moved—so Santa Claus doesn't know our new address," she said, plainly trying to keep her tone soft enough for her son, yet with a slight edge so Lassiter would know he'd asked a thoughtless question. He felt like a jerk.

"Mama says Santa Claus will find us next year—if we don't move." His big, wet eyes met Lassiter's. "But we might have to."

Blast me to Hades for being a stupid idiot! With difficulty he managed to hold on to his grin, while inside he swore he would make it up to Pedro and his mother. "Do you like magic, Pedro?" he asked.

The child nodded, his expression brightening a little.

"Me too." He reached into his jeans pocket and pulled out a coin. "I can make this quarter disappear." With a little slight of hand he'd learned during his less than scholarly first year at Harvard, he directed Pedro's mind away from his grief. "Where did it go?" he asked, showing the boy both of his fists. "Can you guess which hand it's in?"

The boy touched Lassiter's left fist, which he opened to reveal an empty palm. "No. Guess again."

Pedro then touched Lassiter's right fist. Again Lassiter obliged the child, opening his hand to reveal that it, too, was empty. "The quarter's gone!"

The boy looked baffled, which was the point, since it was supposed to be magic. He allowed a pregnant pause, then said, "What's this?" he reached out and touched the boy's ear.

"Why, here it is!" He brought the quarter forward for Pedro to see. "Now how did it get there?"

The "coin in the ear" trick was easy and so old it creaked, but from the surprise and delight on the four-year-old's face, Lassiter was clearly the greatest living wizard in Pedro Rodriguez's world. "Merry Christmas, Pedro." Placing the coin in the boy's hand, he stood up. "And don't worry about Santa. He's smart. He'll find a great young man like you." Turning to Trisha, he said, "Why don't you take Pedro to find Reggie. I bet his mommy would like a photograph of this handsome young man."

Trisha stared at Lassiter. He could see confusion in her eyes, but when he indicated with a half nod to take the boy away, she stood and grasped his hand. "Do you like to get your picture taken, Pedro?" she asked.

He nodded.

Trisha transferred her smile to Pedro's mother. "Is it okay if I take him?" She pointed to a nearby corner. "We'll be over there in front of the Christmas tree."

"Yes, of course." Mrs. Rodriguez touched her son on the arm. "You can go with the lady. But come right back after the picture."

The boy nodded, then took Trisha's hand, tagging along after her as she made her way toward a spindly pine tree, decorated with strings of popcorn and paper ornaments. When the boy was out of earshot, Lassiter knelt beside his young mother. "I want to apologize for my thoughtless remark about Santa Claus." He reached in his pocket and pulled out a silver money clip, slipping two fifty dollar bills from it. "To make up for it, I'd be grateful if you would give him a Merry Christmas on me."

When the young woman started to protest, he pressed the fifties in her hand and closed her fingers around them. "Before you leave, give the man with the camera your address so I can mail you Pedro's picture." He stood, smiling at her. She looked shell-shocked. "Okay?" he asked.

She nodded mutely, the hand that he'd pressed the money into still outstretched. He gently took her wrist and lowered the hand to her lap. "I'm sorry for your loss." He squeezed her shoulder. "You have a great little boy, Mrs. Rodriguez."

She blinked back more tears. "Thank you," she whispered.

Feeling peculiarly inexpert and out of his element, he slid his hands into his pockets. "Well, if you'll excuse me, I'm on dish washing duty." He nodded a farewell and turned away, heading toward the shelter's kitchen.

He had a feeling little Pedro Rodriguez would forget Lassiter Dragan long before the boy's big, sad eyes would fade from his own memory. Not being a man who permitted sentimentality to creep into his day, that realization shook him.

Trisha stood beside Reggie as he snapped several photographs of Pedro. Some splendid human being had hung a dozen or so candy canes on the tree. Coaxing Pedro to smile brightly into the camera had required very little. Just a prized candy treat clutched in each fist. It never ceased to amaze Trisha how little kindness it took, sometimes, to give a person a Merry Christmas.

Unable to help herself, Trisha had glanced back at Lassiter several times as he'd knelt again to speak with Pedro's mother. His expression solemn, compassionate, he'd been gentle. Sympathetic. Trisha still reeled at how sensitively Lassiter had behaved with the tragic little boy—and that magic trick! Who would have guessed Lassiter Dragan could pull a quarter from a four-year-old's ear. How darling was that?

And the way he'd stood at the door from noon until after six o'clock in the evening, passing out meal tickets and coffee, uncomplaining, greeting each destitute wayfarer with a smile or a kind word. Again, who would have guessed?

She had to say it, even if it was only inside her head. She was deeply affected by what she'd seen today. Dangerously charmed. He'd been gallant, friendly and if not dead keen on the idea when she'd proposed it, he'd gone along, chivalrously, without a single grumble. Except about the pie. She couldn't help smiling at that memory. He'd been kidding. He was awfully cute when he kidded.

Hold on a second, there, girlie! an inner voice shouted,

halting her leap into a full-blown Lassiter Dragan flight of fantasy. *Don't lose your mind, just because it's Christmas Day and the guy hasn't decreed "off with her head." For one thing, that Christmas dinner he let you give away is a negligible dent in his budget—and a tax write-off, to boot! Plus, it makes him look like a prince among men for the magazine story. Why shouldn't his good-guy performance ring true? He's got nothing to lose and a lot of positive press to gain!*

The gut-punch reality check wiped the goofy smile off her face.

"Anything wrong?"

Reggie's question caught her off guard. Avoiding direct eye contact, she said, "Not a thing. Thanks for doing this."

"No problem. Happy to do it."

He did seem happy. Trisha wondered at that. Why would he and Jane give up Christmas with their families for these puff stories each year? They didn't seem like the type who cared about the money. But this wasn't the time to ask. Regrouping her emotions, she focused on little Pedro. "Okay, sweetie," she said as brightly as she could manage. "Let's go back to mama." She took the child's hand. Against her will, her gaze shot to the place she had last seen Lassiter. He was gone.

Her foolish heart twisted with regret.

CHAPTER TEN

THE day at the shelter had been long and tiring, but the show must go on! After soaking in a hot bath and changing into a cozy velour lounging outfit, Trisha gamely vacated the dressing room off the bathroom, to join Lassiter in the master's suite. He stood before the hearth, staring into the fire. His hair was still damp from the shower, and he'd changed into fresh black trousers and a white cable knit sweater that made his shoulders look so broad it was cruel.

Ever since they'd entered the bedroom thirty minutes before, the silence had been strained, conversation limited to monosyllables. Trisha knew why she was stressed. The unwelcome attraction she'd felt for him all day weighed heavily on her mind. She didn't know what his problem was. Well, unless you counted the fact that she'd hijacked his Christmas plans. That could do it. Apparently all that seeming good cheer at the shelter had been for show, because he certainly wasn't cheerful now.

When she joined him before the fire, he took her hand without comment, and they strolled down the sweeping staircase, a reasonable facsimile of happy newlyweds.

Joining Reggie, Jane and Perrier in the comfortable seating area before the living room fire, they shared a light meal of crabmeat salads, followed by silky-smooth lemon tarts and coffee. The chatter with Reggie and Jane was friendlier, more natural than it had been at first. Trisha guessed their time at the shelter had put the magazine couple more at ease. Maybe they felt Mr. and Mrs. Dragan, the wealthy venture capitalist and his designer-clothes-wearing bride, were less snooty and stuffy than they'd given them credit for. Trisha was glad they seemed able to relax, since she liked them. She really would love being their friend, but sadly, the lie she and Lassiter were living prevented that.

After the dishes were cleared away, Lassiter and Trisha exchanged gifts before the towering blue spruce, perfectly and opulently decorated. The contrast between today at the shelter and tonight in Lassiter's mansion was—well like the difference between night and day.

Trisha had a hard time retaining her Christmas spirit, but forced a smile for the photographs, her heart growing heavier and heavier with every gift she opened—diamond jewelry, exorbitantly expensive perfume, silks and laces—all breathtaking deceptions that were of little interest or importance to her, even if by some freak chance Lassiter actually meant for her to keep them. All she could think about was how much good these expensive baubles could do, *if* what they cost had been donated to the homeless people that she and her temporary husband helped feed today. Little Pedro loomed in her mind's eye. The memory brought with it a rush of helpless sadness she had difficulty masking behind a lighthearted smile.

The evening wore on like a bizarre dream. Her most vivid recollection was when Lassiter helped fasten a stunning diamond choker about her neck. His hands were warm against her flesh and he smelled nice. She battled a desire to lean back against his chest and nuzzle her cheek against his throat.

It was at crazy, surreal moments like these she had to be especially tough with herself, calling forcefully to mind that his interest in her was *only* as a means to a profitable end. She told herself she must feel exactly the same way. He was the means to a profitable end for her, too. Period.

End of story!

When Lassiter opened gifts that were supposedly *from* her, Trisha looked on in a fog of astonishment. They were too expensive for Trisha to have ever considered purchasing. Lassiter's secretary must have called fancy stores, had salespeople select appropriate items, gift wrap them, script fitting sentiments on parchment enclosure cards, then deliver them to his home—in the nick of time—to be placed beneath the tree by his serving staff. All very correct and cold.

The evening went off without a hitch—except for the one in Trisha's heart. Even for a fifty-thousand dollar loan at prime rate, she felt desolate, dirty. There was so much to abhor about this man's philosophy of life. So much that reminded her of her father. Still, observing Lassiter today at the shelter, witnessing his displays of benevolence and sympathy, she couldn't shake off a wayward fondness for him.

How big a fool did that make her? She, of all people, knew his act at the shelter had been just that—an act for the article. She'd witnessed his shocked expression, his speechless aversion, to the idea of donating his Christmas meal to the homeless. And afterward, she'd observed his silent brooding once they were again ensconced inside the master suite. So why couldn't she rid herself of the soft, gooey feeling whenever she looked at him? Being unable to answer that question annoyed, angered and frustrated her. She wanted to slam out onto the bedroom balcony and scream out her misery to the high heavens.

Deep in the night, she could no longer stand her sleepless imprisonment in Lassiter's bedroom. Was it really possible to detect his scent? He was a good ten feet away. She didn't want to be reminded of him with every restless breath. Why did it seem as though even the light fixtures gave off his scent, their singular aim to taunt her?

She peeked at Perrier, sleeping soundly on the bed in the empty place where a spouse would normally sleep—in a marriage that wasn't purely business. Though moonlight illuminated the room, she had neither the heart nor the emotional strength to peek at Lassiter. She only knew she had heard no sounds from the couch in an eternity, so she decided he must be asleep. If she planned to escape, the time was now.

Stealthily, she crept from the bed, grabbing up the gossamer negligee wrap and slipping it over her gown as she crossed to the door. It wasn't much cover, but just in case Reggie was still up at this hour watching a soccer match from some far off continent, she would be moderately decent when she mumbled an excuse and fled. Since it was after three, she prayed he had finally gone to bed. If she didn't vent some of her pent-up energy she would be forced to scream, and screaming tended to startle people awake. Which was the last thing she wanted to do.

Soundlessly she opened the bedroom door, then closed it behind her, grateful the Dragan home didn't have squeaky hinges or creaky floorboards. At the top of the staircase, she stilled, listening for telltale sounds of TV sports. All was silent. She breathed a long sigh and hurried down the stairs. During Lassiter's Christmas Eve party, she'd made good use of her wandering and found, to her great amazement, an indoor swimming pool set in a domed enclosure made entirely of glass panes. Filled with striking, flowering shrubs and ornamental trees, planted in huge china pots, it had looked like a botanical garden. As she'd entered, she'd expected to pay admission.

Since the pool was housed in glass, it was like being outside, except for the vast, sparkling panorama of snow in all directions. Though the pool and the air were heated and the humidity high, the glass dome didn't fog up. At the time, she'd wondered what miracle caused that. Now, however, the phenomenon of fogless glass wasn't her biggest priority. She only cared about the room's tranquillity and its springtime-in-winter appeal.

She needed a safe haven to alleviate her stress, and a good hard swim was perfect for that. She loved to swim. The only impediment in her plan was that she hadn't purchased a swimsuit during her Vegas shopping spree. She cast off the worry as trivial. The room might be glass, but prying eyes were held at bay behind tall walls, acres and acres away, hidden by snow-crested woodlands.

And at this hour, everyone in the house was asleep. Who would ever know?

Moonlight bathed the pool room in ghostly light, enough to see the shimmer of water, the low diving board, clusters of cushy lounging furniture set in groupings around the pool and beneath towering vegetation.

With the moon turning leaves and flowers to sterling, and silver-gilt foliage casting large sections of the room in shade as black and thick as velvet, the scene was both tranquil and bewitching. Breathing deeply of warm, moist air, scented with the light perfume of flowering plants, Trisha padded over slightly roughened tiles to the closest lounge chair. She discarded her wrap, then shucked her gown, adding it to the pile of baby-blue silk and Belgian lace.

Lassiter had been lying in the darkness for a long time trying not to think. Trying to sleep. It hadn't been working the way he'd told himself to make it work. He'd been thinking a blue streak and he hadn't even been able to close his damn eyes.

He'd glared at the night sky for hours, ticking off the seconds by the pounding in his brain. With each painful thud Lassiter cursed the moon and its dead-slow trip through a twinkling field of stars. The glass-domed pool room was the only place in the house where he could torture himself that way. Exactly why he felt watching the moon travel from one end of heaven to the other was so essential was a mystery. It only proved how little sleep he was getting—proved it in interminable moon minutes, as the contrary orb inched through the sky with the speed of a traffic jam.

On the other hand, watching the moon drag itself through the sky was less painful than sleeping so near Trisha. Tonight he'd had a quick, unintentional glimpse of her as she'd come out of the bathroom in that wispy excuse for pajamas. Even with the matching robe, it had to have been made out of spider webs or invisible kitchen wrap. He'd seen traces of flesh beneath the flimsy fabric, of a lush, lithe body, of womanly contours that made his mouth water and his gut tighten with urges that had nothing to do with their business deal.

As soon as she'd turned her back and settled in, he'd quietly thrown off his covers and left the room. He didn't know if she'd heard him or not, but she hadn't reacted. Taking a serpentine route through his house, he managed to avoid Reggie, watching TV in the den, and ended up in the pool room cursing the moon and himself.

During the last four hours, he'd told himself over and over that he and Trisha had made their deal. Nothing had changed.

Maybe she was sexier than he'd imagined she'd be, and maybe sleeping in the same room with her was becoming more troubling than he'd contemplated. He was a man of his word. He had assured her in no uncertain terms that if she would help him out and agree to the marriage, it would be nonsexual.

Nonsexual!

He was beginning to hate that word, and himself. He was not a weak man. He was not a sex maniac. He was just—well, there was simply something about the woman. Something about her that pushed buttons. Her silly, crooked nose for one thing. Then there was her ridiculously inviting hair, shiny and fragrant, swaying wantonly about her face and shoulders. Worse yet was her smile, when it was real and turned on him. Not to mention his recent, chance glimpse of too tempting flesh.

And then there was the kiss. He let out a long, slow breath. Though he'd tried, damn him, he hadn't been able to forget the excitement, the heat, the crazy, wanton purity of it that had shaken him to his core and drilled its memory so deep in his brain, he could never dig it out. Lots of buttons pushed, hammered, adding up to a big turn-on he was having difficulty killing off.

So here he was, flat on his back, staring at the sky telling himself he could do this. How many more nights? Six. He ground his teeth and bit off a curse. Six? Why did six nights suddenly seem like a couple of million light-years? Where was his celebrated cool, calm detachment? *Get a grip, Dragan! Six nights isn't even a week!*

A sound, like the noise the diving board made when someone bounced on it, brought him out of his troubled musings. He turned toward the deep end. Someone stood near the end of the plank, bobbing up and down, apparently testing its springiness. He sat bolt upright, staring in astonishment. *Blast!* The very female who had driven him to this insane moon vigil stood there—in the most emotionally incendiary way possible. *Naked.*

In the moonlight, her pale skin practically aglow, Trisha jumped and landed, jumped and landed. With seductive grace, her body scandalously defied gravity, then obeyed it, then defied it again. Lassiter hunched forward, damning the fates for their heinous prank when he was already teetering on the brink of madness.

Dive, damn it, *dive!* he commanded inside his head, knowing if he said anything aloud, he would humiliate her to the point that she would leave, and the game would be up. So he hunkered there in pain, mentally shouting *dive,* like some submarine commander straining to save his boat and his crew from imminent annihilation.

The analogy wasn't far from the truth. He felt like any second he might explode.

At long last, she sprang into the air. Arms outstretched, she arched aloft, floated in midair for a moment, like an angel, before executing a perfect swan dive, leaving hardly a ripple where her body disappeared beneath the surface.

Lassiter felt bruised and battered, anger and desire skewering him. He sat doubled over, his body stiff, sluggish. Luckily, his brain functioned on all cylinders, flashing a red alert. *Get the hell out, Dragan! Get out now, before you do something stupid!*

He rose up, growling, more animal than man. The savage inside him told him to dive in, grab her and take her right there, right now. But the other part of him, the civilized being who'd made her a promise, ultimately prevailed.

When Trisha came up for air she was alone, never knowing how close she came to encountering a not-so-gentlemanly dragon.

CHAPTER ELEVEN

When Trisha woke in the morning, she peeked at Lassiter, surprised to find him sitting up, running his hands through his hair. Muscles in his arms and chest flexed, drawing her wayward gaze.

"Good morning." She sat up, clutching blankets before her for modesty. "Sleep well?"

If she thought he had been moody last night, she didn't know when she'd been well off. He peered at her with the most annoyed expression she'd ever seen. "Yeah—great," he ground out. "And you?"

"Not so well." She decided a little truth was in order. "I— went for a swim. I hope you don't mind."

He clenched his jaw, his irritation unmistakable. It throbbed in the air like a pounding heart. "Mind?" he asked, his voice tight. "Why should I mind?"

She was confused by his open hostility. "Are you still mad at me for giving away your Christmas dinner?"

"Ancient history," he said, gruffly.

"Then what's the matter? What have I done to make you so angry?"

"I'm not angry." He shoved up from the sofa. She was relieved to notice he had on navy boxer shorts. "I'm going to take a shower."

"Mind if I go down to breakfast? I showered after I swam."

"Yeah, I know," he muttered, crossing by the foot of the bed.

"You what?"

He clenched his fists, and stalked toward the bathroom. "I said—fine. Go."

"Oh…"

He slammed the bathroom door behind him. For a long time

she sat there, bewildered. "Well…" she said at last, patting Perrier. "It's obvious Mr. Dragan regrets his bargain with us." She sighed, feeling depressed. "I guess we both have our regrets."

The mutt watched her with such unquestioning love and loyalty she managed a smile. Lifting her pet in her arms, she scrambled out of the bed. "It's only for a few more days. Then we'll both have what we want and we can forget…" The sentence died, too laughably untrue to voice aloud. At least on her part.

Lassiter Dragan would forget this holiday inconvenience—sharing his home and his life with her. But she had a nagging feeling she wouldn't be that lucky. "We *will* forget him," she whispered sternly to Perrier. The dog yapped, cocking her head, as though highly dubious. "Look," Trisha admonished softly, "don't I have enough problems without you calling me a liar?"

Trisha dressed hurriedly and met Reggie and Jane in the dining room. They both looked fresh and well-rested. Though Jane was naturally quiet and shy she had loosened up somewhat and the threesome chatted like old friends. Trisha learned that they both looked forward to these "Home for the Holidays" jaunts. Neither had family, so they'd volunteered to cover the first one, four years ago. The series became instantly popular. They continued to take on the job, allowing other magazine writers and photographers to spend the holidays with family.

Reggie and Jane told her they liked working for the *Sophisticate* well enough, but both had loftier goals. Reggie hoped one day to become a wilderness photographer, like Ansel Adams, and Jane admitted with a blush, that when not writing puff pieces for the magazine, she was a struggling playwright.

Though Jane was a quiet egghead and Reggie a free-and-easy hippie, Trisha suspected they were attracted to each other, but insecure about declaring themselves. She sensed they each feared their feelings were one-sided, and to reveal them would ruin a good working relationship.

Lassiter finally appeared, disturbingly attractive in jeans and a gray V-neck sweater. He brushed Trisha's cheek affectionately with his knuckles, as a new bridegroom might, and took a seat at her side. Not expecting his caress, Trisha's blush was real. So was her answering smile, but not because she delighted in Lassiter's touch, which, tragically, she did. She smiled because she'd made a decision she felt good about. Jane and Reggie didn't know it, but they now had their own, personal matchmaker.

"Sledding!" she said, drawing everyone's perplexed attention.

"What?" Lassiter asked.

"I said, sledding. I think we should go." She indicated the dining room's tall, arched window, showcasing the snowy panorama outside, dazzling in the morning sun. "It's a beautiful winter day." She turned to her holiday husband and beamed. "We do have sleds, don't we, darling?"

"I've got a couple in the garage."

"Wonderful." She slid her chair away from the table. "I'm for a day of sledding. Anybody want to join me?"

She knew that any devoted bridegroom would have to say yes. And since Reggie and Jane were doing the article about Lassiter, they, too, would need to go. So very soon, appropriately clothed for snow, Trisha, Lassiter, Jane and Reggie, with his ever-ready camera, trudged toward the property's best sledding hill.

The trek was exhilarating, the day crisp and still, the world covered in an icing of white. She told herself the fact that Lassiter held her gloved hand as they plodded through calf-deep snow didn't enter into the excitement at all. Still, she was more breathless than she should have been, since most of the distance was over level ground. And her cheeks were strangely hot, considering the temperature was well below freezing.

"What brought on this sudden passion for sledding?" Lassiter asked.

Trisha looked back over her shoulder at the couple from the magazine. They lagged only a car length behind, so she whispered, "For Reggie and Jane. I'm matchmaking."

"You're what?" Lassiter was cute when he frowned in confusion, darn him.

His query had been a little too loud and she gave him a cautioning stare. "It's obvious they're crazy about each other."

"Not to me."

"Well, you're not exactly Mr. Sensitivity, are you?"

After a couple of beats, he admitted, "It's not my area of expertise, no."

"Well then…" Sensing Reggie and Jane were catching up, she smiled broadly. "You'll have to take my word—darling."

Lassiter flicked a glance over his shoulder, flashing a sexy grin that made her heart trip over itself. "Whatever you say, sweetheart."

"What are you two whispering about?" Reggie called.

"She was propositioning me." Lassiter's gaze capturing hers. Did she see a cunning twinkle in his eyes? "I told her it wasn't that kind of magazine article."

Reggie's laughter rang in the pines. Trisha lowered her focus to the snow. Her face, already warm, now practically blazed.

"This is it," Lassiter said with a sweep of his arm to display the long, downhill vista before them. The slope was dotted sparsely with pines and pin oaks, the valley below at least a football field length away. It didn't look terribly hazardous or steep. She wondered if he'd paid to have the perfect sledding hill created on his property, then shook off the silly notion. "It—it looks—quite sledable," she said.

"I'm gratified you approve, my love."

His love. She swallowed hard. *His love.* The endearment he spoke so glibly for their company caused a prick of pain in her chest. She didn't want to be his love, but to hear him say it—having the words sound so real—well, it had a strange, melancholy effect, like some stupid part of her wanted it to be true.

"Great sledding hill!" Reggie said as he and Jane tromped to the brink of the slope.

Trisha worked to boost herself out of the emotional hole

she seemed so willing to languish in lately. "My sentiments exactly."

Since her matchmaking plan was to get Jane and Reggie together on a sled, she grasped too late that she and Lassiter must share the other. She eyed the spindly, wooden conveyances. They looked awfully small, especially if they were going to hold two adults.

"So—so how do we ride these things?" she asked. The sledding idea had been rather spur of the moment. The last time she'd been on one they'd seemed huge. If she remembered correctly, there'd been three or four of her pals on one with her.

Reggie hung his camera on the low branch of a pine. "The guys lie down and gals get on top."

This announcement came as a significant shock to Trisha. "I've never ridden on a sled lying down." She was troubled by the notion of climbing on top of Lassiter and—and, well, clinging to the full length of him. "What about sitting. If I remember right, I—I used to do it sitting."

"That's another way." Reggie climbed on the sled and lay on his stomach, motioning Jane over. "You can sit in the front and Lassiter can straddle you."

"Um—straddle me?" she echoed, her tone making it clear she wasn't totally on board with that method either.

"Yeah, only you'll be less aerodynamic that way."

"What do you suggest, sweetheart?" Lassiter asked, sounding vaguely amused. "Standing on the thing?"

She gave him a perturbed look. "Well, snow borders stand up, don't they?"

Lassiter leaned down, slid her knit cap off one ear and nibbled at the lobe, startling her so badly she would have sunk to her knees if he hadn't encircled her shoulders with his arm. "We're supposed to be married," he warned softly between nibbles. "Sledding was your idea, so either lie on top of me or ride between my legs. Your choice."

Her adrenaline level shot up, every nerve in her body leaping and shuddering. How could he make a little innocent sledding sound so lewd?

"Are you two going to stand there all day propositioning each other?" Reggie asked with a leer. "Or are you going sledding?"

Lassiter straightened, but kept his arm about her, which was a good thing, since her knees were the consistency of jelly. She pulled her knit cap back over her ear and worked at steadying her breathing. "S-sledding…" The word came out an octave high, so she cleared her throat.

Jane settled on top of Reggie, her cheek on his parka between his shoulder blades. She smiled shyly. Trisha could tell the young woman was thrilled to have an excuse to hold on to the photographer. Even though the tingle of Lassiter's earlobe-nibbling still buzzed through her veins, she managed a smile, meaning it. She decided she could deal with being on the same sled with Lassiter, since it was for a such good cause. She motioned for Lassiter to get on. "Lie down, darling. We wouldn't want to be less aerodynamic."

"I know I wouldn't." His tone taunted, but she ignored it. He knelt, then lay flat on their sled, eyeing her with wry amusement. "Isn't it marvelous how much alike we think?"

"Astonishing," Trisha said, as she watched Jane close her eyes and take a deep breath, relishing Reggie's scent. Trisha didn't have to have a house fall on her to be positive she was doing the right thing, no matter how much torture she might have to endure personally.

"Ready, sweetheart?" Lassiter's question held a slight edge, a vague warning, reminding her that she was supposed to be his bride, not some squeamish virgin afraid of a man's touch. He eyed her narrowly.

She got the message and clambered on his back. "Ready, willing and able—*lover*," she said, a little too determinedly.

"Wanna race?" Reggie asked, pushing off.

"No—uh—"

"You're on," Lassiter cut in.

The remainder of Trisha's refusal became a shriek of panic when he shoved off, and they were instantly hurtling downhill. She clutched him, holding on for dear life.

After her initial terror subsided, Trisha found the ride intoxicating. Like Jane, she closed her eyes, breathed deeply of Lassiter's scent as they sped into the valley. She heard squeals and laughter and realized Reggie and Jane had tumbled. Trisha was elated to see them tangled together, clinging to each other.

When their own sled came to a halt, she indicated the other couple. "They'll be engaged by New Year's Day."

"You're a hopeless romantic," Lassiter said.

She didn't think being a hopeless romantic was a bad thing, but he made it sound like a failing, and that made her mad. "I'd rather be a hopeless romantic than plain hopeless," she retorted under her breath, "...like you, Mr. Quid pro quo!"

"Your opinion of me is noted, Miss August." He shifted his shoulders in a way that made her sway from side to side. "You might want to get off. It's hard to take a sled up a hill in this position."

"Oh..." She felt like an idiot, lying on top of him, arguing. She scrambled off the sled onto her knees in the snow. Reggie and Jane were still in a heap, seeming to be in no hurry to free themselves. She watched with a pleasure that was maternal—or more correctly, the pleasure of a fairy godmother. A hand at her elbow told her Lassiter was helping her to her feet. She avoided eye contact, but mumbled a thank you.

Their trek up the hill was a quiet one, with neither speaking. On their next ride down, Trisha experienced the same intense gratification, and couldn't decide how much of it was excitement over the ride and how much was due to the fact that she lay on top of Lassiter Dragan.

The morning rushed by in a delirious haze. They laughed and kidded and threw snowballs, sledded down and trudged up the hill a million times. Lassiter was a great sled skipper, never overturning them. On the other hand, Reggie and Jane spent half their time entwined in a heap and loving every minute of it. Trisha suspected a big percentage of their spills were not accidental.

A thought flashed through her mind. An unruly thought. More of a wayward wish—that she and Lassiter would tumble into the snow and get all tangled together. *No, no! Trisha! You want nothing of the sort.*

The next instant, she found herself pitched sideways, flying through the air. She screamed, clutching and clawing for purchase. When she came to rest and her vision cleared, Lassiter lay on his back in the snow and she straddled him. They were nose to nose. How they ended up in that incriminating position, Trisha couldn't guess. Well, she could, but she didn't want to. *Be careful what you wish for, Trisha. You wished for this! Aren't you ashamed!*

"That's a spectacular shot! Kiss her!" Reggie shouted, sounding as though he was racing down the hill.

When Trisha's mind stopped doing cartwheels and she absorbed Reggie's suggestion, she gasped and started to pull away. She couldn't chance another kiss from this man. She was having trouble enough keeping his first kiss from wrecking her judgment.

"No," Lassiter warned, slipping his arms about her. "He's right. It's time."

She stared, bewildered by his cryptic remark. *It's time?* "But—but he's already taken a picture of us kiss—"

"Enough!" Lassiter's hard-edged whisper allowed no debate. He pulled her down. For such a frigid day, his mouth felt surprisingly warm against hers. She found herself reveling in his heat, all resistance melting away like a hapless snowflake that might have been caught between his lips and hers.

His kiss was a sensuous, primeval act of mastery. He seemed to be saying, *"I am man and you are my woman."* Oh, how beautifully his lips lied—propelling her to the very threshold of belief, even though she, of all people, knew the truth.

Trisha was stunned senseless, inflamed and frightened in equal parts. Lassiter's kiss provoked, taunted, burned like wildfire. She wondered if he could possibly be as affected as she? If her womanly intuition was any judge at all, the lingering caress of his mouth certainly told the story that way.

His lips moved provocatively, fostering breathtaking, primal sensations. She felt herself losing control—with this near stranger—while pictures were being snapped. A mind-bending dementia was overwhelming her, spreading through her veins like some incurable love virus.

The word *love* hit her—hard. *No! No! This man is a business partner! Nothing more!* She must not allow herself to succumb, for she sensed deep in her heart there would be no hope for a cure.

She shoved against his chest, the act a silent plea to end this dishonesty—*now*—before she tumbled over a precipice that would leave her broken and bloodied in the abyss of Lassiter's cast-offs.

"Great! Cool!" Reggie shouted. "What a shot! Lovers in the snow. It doesn't get better than this!"

Lassiter's hands slid from her back, releasing her. She opened her eyes to find herself gazing directly into his—narrow and guarded, giving nothing away.

Lassiter sat in one of the four cane and wicker chairs stationed at the eating bar on one side of the kitchen's center island. He stared unseeing at the counter-high fireplace in the exterior wall. Firelight flickered, casting its ghostly shadows on the arched, brick and granite surround, the rustic, beamed ceiling, pine cabinetry and trendy farmhouse sink.

The firelight was all that illuminated the room as he sat, stock-still, a mug of cooling coffee in front of him on the slate countertop. He didn't feel like being in the light right now. He needed darkness to go with his mood.

He was furious with himself. He could have kissed Trisha for the article without all the heat, damn him. What had come over him out there in the blasted snow? Sure, all morning he'd watched Reggie and Jane grope each other in the name of innocent play, and yes, it had begun to wear him down. Especially when he had to endure the stirring pressure of Trisha's soft, femininity along his back and legs, every time they sledded down the hill.

And yes, he had overturned their sled on purpose. It had been a temporary lapse in judgment. He covered his face with his hands, admitting to himself the lapse hadn't been all that temporary. He'd not only wrecked the sled, but he'd gone on to drag Trisha down and kissed her like he intended to seduce her there in the snow, not like he wanted a magazine to *think* he planned to seduce her. There was a difference, and the difference was intent. His intent had been to seduce, not simply to imply a seduction.

He bit off a curse. He'd wanted to seduce her. He might have, if there hadn't been an audience. That made him furious with himself. He didn't want to feel passionate about Trisha August. At least not the kind of passion that involved an emotional connection.

His own family had left him with no warm, fuzzy feelings about the institution of marriage. Women were better left for temporary pleasure, nothing long-term, since long-term relationships could turn to ice, benumbing emotional closeness. "The value of family is highly overrated," he muttered.

"You're so wrong," came a familiar, female voice.

He sensed more than saw a light coming on. When he lowered his hands from his eyes, the kitchen was flooded with illumination. Wincing at the unwelcome brightness, he turned to see Trisha standing in the doorway, one hand on her hip and a contrary look her face. "Evening," he said without smiling. Why must she look sexy in baggy gray sweats, her hair hanging straight, still wet from the shower. He held up his mug. "Want some coffee?"

She nodded. "I'll get it."

He watched her take a mug down from a cabinet and pour herself a cup. She walked up beside him and plunked her coffee on the counter next to his. "Don't you want to know why you're wrong?"

He could detect her shampoo, orange blossoms with a hint of citrus. Lounging back, he shifted to better see her, resting an arm along the back of his chair. "Not particularly."

She smirked, lifted a hand and quirked a finger at him. "Come with me."

He frowned.

She cocked her head toward the door. "It'll only take a second." She hooked his little finger with hers, tugging. "Come on."

He eyed her grimly, but got up and followed her to the doorway where she stopped him. "Look." She pointed into the den where Jane sat cross-legged on the rug, playing with Perrier before the hearth. The sound of her giggle floated across the distance as she and Trisha's pet played tug-of-war with a sock.

Reggie knelt nearby, taking their picture. With the flash of the camera, Jane lifted her gaze to Reggie. The couple shared a quiet smile.

"See?"

"What?" Lassiter knew the answer, but decided not to destroy Trisha's pleasure in telling him. Clearly today's outing had turned a corner in the relationship between Reggie and Jane. The change was apparent in the way they looked at each other, the way they smiled. Since coming in from the snow they'd seemed to always be touching, brushing, needing a physical connection. It was a curious phenomenon, watching people fall in love.

Trisha motioned toward the kitchen's center island. "Come on."

He followed her, seating himself where he'd been before.

"You think the value of family is overrated?" She waved toward the kitchen door. "How about the value to two lonely people who won't be lonely anymore?"

"There's that hopeless romantic coming out again," he taunted.

She eyed him reproachfully. "Just because your parents were a couple of ice cubes doesn't mean everybody's marriage is unhappy."

Ice cubes. A fitting description. Either she was very intuitive or she believed only ice cubes could have conceived him. It wasn't particularly flattering that she thought of him as cold, especially since she provided the other set of lips for the kiss they'd shared, today—a kiss he'd found to be extremely hot. *She's your business partner, Dragan, not your girlfriend,* he reproached inwardly. *Her opinion of your kiss is immaterial to your deal!* "From what you said of your early childhood, your family wasn't perfect," he said, masking his beleaguered mental state with a reasonable tone. "Why this fiery defense of family life?"

"Because, I also saw how happy my mother was when she finally remarried. Her second husband wasn't anything like my dad. He was caring, sweet, and loved mom unconditionally. That's why I believe, with the right man, marriage can be wonderful."

He refused to argue the point. She could think whatever she wanted. He was tired, stressed and more than a little provoked that she could stand there in shapeless sweats, looking down her crooked little nose, and turn him on. "Then isn't it lucky that we're already married?" he quipped, then recoiled inwardly. Where had that come from? Isn't it lucky? *Lucky?* Was he nuts?

Her smirk froze, then slowly disappeared.

The answer to his question was clear. She didn't have to say a word for him to see she would walk barefoot for miles over broken glass rather than contemplate anything more meaningful than their disposable marriage. Unfortunately, he sensed she didn't plan to let his query slide without a few pointed remarks.

She lifted her chin and rebelliously met his gaze. "There are two kinds of luck, Mr. Dragan." Her voice had grown hushed and hard. "As a profit and loss junky, yourself, I think you can sense which column I'd put our marriage in!"

CHAPTER TWELVE

THE morning of December twenty-seventh, Trisha got a break from the unrelenting pull of Lassiter Dragan's charisma. Reggie and Jane went with him to the Dragan building for a tour. Though the article was basically about how he spent the Christmas holidays, Reggie felt it necessary to visit the Dragan building, take some pictures, since Lassiter's success as a venture capitalist was what brought him to the attention of *The Urban Sophisticate* in the first place.

Trisha ate breakfast alone. She watched snow fall as a servant hovered, ready to grant her every wish. After sitting there for nearly an hour, she vaulted up, grabbed her mug and headed for the kitchen. The servant trailed after her, declaring she need only ask and coffee would be brought to her. Trisha waved off the man. "Trust me. I've had lots of experience serving coffee."

Her mug refilled, Trisha noticed a stack of Christmas cards on the kitchen desk. Curious, she scrutinized the stack as she sipped. She knew another person's mail was none of her business. But somehow, Christmas cards seemed different, less forbidden. After all, they were meant to be displayed and enjoyed.

With that rationalization firmly in her head, she carried the stack into the den and curled on the Oriental rug to go through them. Perrier joined her there and she patted the mutt's fuzzy head. "Who do you suppose is on Lassiter's holiday card list?" she murmured. "He seems like such a loner, but he gets a lot of Christmas cards."

Many greetings were from businesses, which didn't surprise Trisha. Some were from individuals, including the governor and a couple of well-known senators; more than a few were from single women. But the most surprising thing of all was how many cards had come from charities, thanking Lassiter for his generous donations. One in particular caught her eye. It mentioned a college scholarship that Lassiter sponsored for deserving young people.

"What do you know, Perrier?" she said, holding up the greeting card to admire its golden embossed artwork. "Mr. Dragan is a giver. Who would have thought?" Her father had given reluctantly to charity, if at all.

Thumbing through the cards once more, she decided to string them around for a more festive look. Though Lassiter's home was beautifully decorated, it lacked hominess. With help from the butler and housekeeper, Trisha gathered red ribbon, scissors, tape and a stepladder. An hour later she'd festooned the double-doored entry to the great room with a fringe of holiday greeting cards.

When Lassiter, Reggie and Jane returned, Trisha happened to be standing in the entry to the great room, framed by her handiwork. She froze, feeling as though she'd been caught in the commission of a crime. *Don't be ridiculous!* she told herself. *What do you care what Lassiter thinks? It's practically a sin to tuck away lovely holiday cards in a dark cubbyhole when they could be out, delighting the eye.*

He came to an abrupt halt, his expression making it clear something was amiss. He'd worn a suit to the office, so standing there in the entryway, Lassiter Dragan was a textbook example of "tall, dark and handsome." Melting snowflakes twinkled on his shoulders. She fought off a silly, schoolgirl light-headedness and held out her arms. *"Ta da!"* she said with a hopeful grin. "It's a little late, but don't they look cheerful?"

Reggie took a picture. "Nice homey touch."

She blessed him for the dear man he was. "My sentiments exactly!" Her gaze skittered to Lassiter as he eyed the kaleidoscopic array. Her stomach fluttered. She hated the realization that his opinion mattered as much as it seemed to. "What do you think—darling?"

His slow grin might or might not have been the real article. "Very homey," he said.

That could mean he actually liked it, or it could be code for "very tacky." She couldn't tell. "My mom and I decorated around doorways with our holiday cards," she said, knowing if she weren't careful she'd be babbling. "I—I miss that, so I decided, why not carry on the tradition!" *Stop now! Shut up!* She bit the inside of her cheek to make sure she said nothing else.

"Traditions are important." Jane flipped to a new page in her notebook and scribbled.

Trisha had a bad feeling that whether Lassiter approved or not, this holiday potpourri of cards would end up on the pages of *The Urban Sophisticate,* perhaps instead of a shot of his fancy office. Drat! That made one more reason for him to be upset with her—tackying up his home for all the world to see. She strained to hang on to her smile. "Um—er—Marvin said to tell you lunch will be ready in twenty minutes." She clasped her hands together, trying to appear the hospitable hostess. "So there's time, if you care to freshen up."

"Good idea," Reggie said. "I need to get another roll of film and—do a little organizing."

"I think I'll freshen up," Jane said with a small smile and pinkened cheeks.

The couple excused themselves and went up the stairs, side by side. Trisha wondered how much freshening up time they would spend together. She hadn't missed the quick look they'd exchanged. It had been brief but spoke volumes. Well, she was happy for them. How ironic that Reggie and Jane had come to Kansas City to do a story on the newlywed Dragans, but more come-hithering was going on between the interviewers than the interviewees.

Once Trisha was alone with Lassiter, she walked over to him, speaking quietly so they wouldn't be overheard. "I hope you're not angry about the Christmas cards."

He lifted his gaze over her head and seemed to ponder the cards, strung together on a wide, red ribbon. "It's fine," he said without inflection.

She experienced a prick of disappointment. "You could be a little more enthusiastic."

He met her gaze, his lips parting in a cynical half grin. "You went through my mail, Miss August. Be satisfied that I'm not angry."

She could see his point. Just because she'd rationalized in her mind that his Christmas cards weren't really all that personal, didn't make it true. As a private person, he had a right to be furious with her. "Yes, of course, you're right." She turned to glance at the fringe of cards, then faced him again. Wisdom dictated that she drop the subject now, but wise or not, she had to add one more thing. "It's none of my business but, I'd be negligent if I didn't give you the praise you deserve."

Skepticism shadowed his eyes. "Praise? From you?"

"Yes, as hard as it is to believe—praise, from me." She shrugged sheepishly. "I noticed quite a few of the cards were from charities." She smiled, not easy in the face of his distrust. "You and my father may be alike in many ways, but you're far more generous than he ever was. Doing so much good, you must feel the warmest glow inside."

His skeptical expression remained unaltered, as though he didn't think she made much sense. "I feel duty-bound to give back to the community. And donations are a tax write-off." He checked his watch. "When did you say lunch would be served?"

"Noon." She watched him, his eyes, his features, seeing no indication of fulfillment or satisfaction for all his giving.

"If you'll excuse me, I think I'll change before lunch."

"Sure."

He turned away, taking the stairs two at a time. After he was gone, she shook her head. Lassiter Dragan did a great deal of good with his money, but didn't seem to get any emotional boost from it.

"That's so sad," she said to the empty entry hall. Lifting Perrier in her arms, she carried her pet into the den. "A person should get something back from doing good—besides a tax write-off. He should *feel* better. It should make him happy." Of course, feeling and happiness required the free reign of one's emotions, which was a liberty Lassiter did not allow himself.

She sat on the rug in front of the fire, and stared hard into the flames. Was Lassiter really as hopeless a case as she'd first thought? He could have fun, something her father never seemed to have time to do. And Lassiter hadn't harangued on and on about the Christmas dinner give-away, or the fact that he'd spent hours elbow-deep in dishwater.

He'd quietly, gallantly done what had been asked of him. Trisha didn't think her father had ever lifted a finger to help around the house, or given a cent for charity, that he hadn't griped incessantly about afterward.

Lassiter might have a ruthlessly pragmatic bottom-line mentality, but his soul was sound. He deserved to feel exhilarated, joyful over his philanthropy. "Perrier, honey, we'll only be here for a few more days," she whispered, stroking her dog's back. "How can we help Mr. Dragan feel the glow?"

The afternoon had been set aside for an in-depth interview with Lassiter about his family history and childhood. Trisha had to admit she was very interested in how he would describe his family life. But true to Lassiter's reluctance to open up, his story was vague and brief.

She did learn that the picture of the beautiful Spanish lady over the great room's hearth was not merely any old masterpiece, but a portrait of his great-grandmother, Condesa Madelena de la Viña, the original owner of the wedding rings she wore. According to Lassiter, the Condesa and her husband, Conde Diego de la Viña, came to the United States just before the first World War. Trisha would have been intimidated by his blue Spanish blood, if she hadn't already been as intimidated as it was possible for her to be.

When asked about his father's side, he joked that he was descended from Romanian Gypsy fortune-tellers. His grandparents, Melchior and Ida Dragan, came to the U.S.A. as refugees after World War II. Their only son, Johann, was Lassiter's father.

Trisha sat quietly, finding Lassiter's history full of surprises.

Spanish nobility and Romanian Gypsies, of all things. That fanciful melting pot of genes had borne spectacularly successful results, when it came to brains, good looks and business acumen, if not emotional dexterity. She'd thought a mix of Spanish and Gypsy blood would overflow with emotionalism. And from Lassiter's kisses—well, there was *plenty* of fire there. She sensed Lassiter held within him deep wells of passion, if one could only break through the icy crust of his emotional isolation.

Once again, she experienced a pang of compassion. Lassiter needed help to break free, to learn to love and live fully. He had a right to enjoy the good he did, not simply exist in a frozen fog, wearing blinders that only allowed him to see life in sterile columns of profit and loss figures.

As she sat quietly observing the interview, Marvin startled her with a tap on her shoulder. He held out a cordless phone. "A call for you, Mrs. Dragan."

She nodded, took the phone and excused herself, wondering who might be calling her here. She'd told no one where she could be reached, except her landlady, in case of an emergency. What could be wrong? In the entry hall, out of earshot, she said, "Hello?"

"Oh, Trisha," came a harried female voice. "It's Kindra."

"What's wrong?"

"We've got a crisis!" She paused, then added, "Hey, I just realized that—that guy who answered the phone. He called you Mrs. Dragan. What did he mean? Are you—did you get *married?*"

Trisha bit her lip, but knew she had to say something. Kindra wasn't the kind of person to let any news so juicy go until she'd squeezed out ever detail. "Um—well. Actually—yes." After all, it wasn't a lie.

"Oh, my Lord. Oh, my Lord! How? When? I can't believe it!"

Kindra wasn't the only one who couldn't believe it. "There's not much to tell. It was a whirlwind thing."

"Wow, it sounds like a fairy tale." Trisha winced. Kindra didn't know how right she was. "I'm so happy for you. I swear, if I had any other choice I'd hang up right now, but I've already tried everybody! With the holidays and all..." She let the sentence die. "I hate myself for disturbing you on your honeymoon, but I'm absolutely *dying* I'm so desperate! Chuck's had an unexpected money crunch, and can't donate the paint and supplies he promised. And three of our volunteers had to be gone this week. Stuff they didn't anticipate. So we're in deep trouble!" She took a quick breath, sounding on the verge of tears.

Trisha's heart sank. She didn't need this right now. "Don't cry, Kindra."

"Okay—okay." She sniffed, clearly trying to get herself under control. "But it's just that Mrs. Chappell and her girls have to be out of their apartment by the thirty-first. We can't dump them and all their worldly possessions in the snow and say, 'We know it's cold and wet, but it'll only be a week or so. Try not to freeze to death.' Their house absolutely must be ready by New Year's Day. What are we going to do without paint and volunteers? I know you've already done way more than your share, but the plain truth is, we need a miracle!"

Trisha felt sick. She'd gotten to know the Chappell family while she and other Kansas City volunteers helped build their Habitat For Humanity home. She adored Mrs. Chappell, a thirty-four-year-old widow, with three little girls. They'd had it tough. Getting this home would help give them self-respect, security, pride of ownership and a real shot at prosperity. The girls could concentrate on school, on making the grades they would need for college scholarships.

Trisha had been an HFH volunteer with her mom since she'd been old enough to pick up a hammer. She knew how vastly lives could be improved, how far young people could go, if given sound, safe environments.

She wanted to help, but she was only one person, and she sure couldn't afford all that paint, the brushes, drop clothes and everything else Chuck had promised. Chuck Milson, a long-time HFH volunteer, had to be devastated, forced by money problems to renege on his pledge. Her heart went out to him. But what could she do about it? "Um—well, Kindra, to be honest, this really is a bad time to…"

She shook her head, words failing her. What could she tell her distraught friend? That she was in the middle of a temporary marriage to a wealthy venture capitalist so she could get a business loan? And at the moment a writer was interviewing her so-called bridegroom for a puff piece in a national magazine that would be extremely profitable to him? That was why she couldn't be bothered to help a family get into their first real home?

She heard Reggie's horsey guffaw, and wondered what was so funny. She glanced into the great room, saw them, all three, casually enjoying the warmth of a cavernous, blazing hearth. The portrait above the mantel, the aristocratic beauty, Condesa Madelena de la Viña, seemed to be gazing directly at Trisha, smiling at her.

Trisha stared at the image, then at Lassiter and his guests, then back up at the Condesa and her kind, compelling smile. A wild thought formed in her brain, refusing to be dislodged. True, it was wild, but it had potential—in more ways than one.

She smiled back at the regal Spanish lady in the portrait. "Kindra, I have a plan."

CHAPTER THIRTEEN

LASSITER looked around at the group of Habitat For Humanity volunteers, eating pizza, laughing, chattering and relaxing. The pizza parlor employees had dragged five tables together to make one long tabletop to accommodate the twelve tired, paint-spattered workers, plus the Chappell family.

Even after three days of painting all the interior walls and baseboards, Lassiter couldn't quite believe Trisha had actually talked him, Reggie and Jane into helping finish the house before the thirty-first, which was tomorrow. He also couldn't believe he'd actually had fun. He'd grown to like and respect the volunteers, and he liked Mrs. Chappell and her three girls.

He glanced at the family, seated together at the other end of the long table. They were redheads, each with a enough freckles to rival the stars in the universe. And each of them was liberally splotched with "Barely Butterscotch" latex paint, especially the eight-year-old, Emma. She looked like she'd spent a great deal of her time standing under dripping paintbrushes. An irregular pattern of spots stood out like brilliant beacons in her curly, crimson hair. She also boasted a comical Barely Butterscotch mustache and goatee, quickly becoming a base coat for pizza sauce.

The young girl laughed, a high-pitched tinkle easy to pick out above the lower resonance of the adult voices. Lassiter grinned, watching her, so completely happy at that moment. He'd heard bits and pieces of the family's history from Trisha and other volunteers. The Chappell family'd had some hard knocks, the kind little girls shouldn't have to know about, let alone deal with.

Lassiter relaxed back in his chair, so tired he ached in places he didn't even know he had. Even so, it was a good tired. It wasn't the same kind of tired he felt after a strenuous workout at the gym, or the same kind of good feeling he experienced in business, no matter how fruitful the deal may have been. It was different. A *better* different. He couldn't decide why, and was too weary to examine it now. Crossing his arms, he closed his eyes and listened to the merry racket.

As he sat quietly, satiated and mellow, he allowed his mind to drift without coherent thought. He caught snatches of conversation about the Chappell's move tomorrow. Plenty of volunteers had signed up to help with that, so this pizza party was a farewell pig-out for the painting crew. Every so often he could single out Trisha's voice from among the many. As his "bride," she naturally sat at his right hand.

He inhaled deeply, detecting pepperoni, paint and Trisha's perfume, a whimsical blend of lilac and newly mown hay. He quirked a wry grin. Leave it to Trisha to make hay smell sexy.

He felt a sharp poke on his right side, just below his ribcage. Apparently his bride wanted his attention. "There are less painful ways to find out if I'm dead," he said without opening his eyes. "Try holding a mirror to my mouth. Let me know if it clouds up."

"That's the *glow* you're feeling," she whispered.

Her comment didn't make sense. It had nothing to do with what he'd said. After a couple of seconds he peered her way. "Excuse me?"

She smiled, a streak of Barely Butterscotch accenting the crook of her nose. He had a hard time restraining himself from leaning over and kissing that painted proboscis. She had some nerve being so cute and so *verboten*.

"You're feeling the glow of satisfaction," she said. "…of a good deed well done. It's a nice feeling, isn't it?"

He eyed her skeptically. He'd spent years distancing himself from emotionalism, so the idea of glowing didn't sit well. He dismissed the notion as the stuff of fairy tales and chick flicks. He'd volunteered with these people for three days now, and had found them to be interesting and enjoyable. Together they'd worked like dogs. He was exhausted. He wanted to take a shower and fall into bed—er—onto the blasted sofa. If it made Trisha feel better to think of the chemical imbalance that constituted muscle fatigue as some kind of noble glow, that was her problem. "There's that hopeless romantic coming out again," he said. "I'm just tired. We all are."

She made a face that looked more pitying than annoyed. "You can deny it and fight it all you want. But mark my words—*darling*—you felt the glow tonight. Someday you'll admit it and you'll thank me." She lifted her chin, placing her paint-streaked nose in imminent danger of being kissed.

Seized by unruly urge, coupled with the need to jolt the pity from her eyes, he did.

For most of her life, Trisha had celebrated New Year's Eve with other Habitat For Humanity volunteers and their families, at homes of volunteers lucky enough to own homes. Tonight, however, she'd had to beg off. Lassiter had committed them to a completely different kind of New Year's Eve party—a formal affair, being held in a hotel ballroom near Kansas City's fashionable Crown Center. Those in attendance would be the city's social elite. Trisha looked forward to it like oral surgery.

She sat beside Lassiter in his sporty Porsche, Reggie and Jane following behind in the chauffeured limousine. For most of the ride neither Lassiter nor Trisha spoke. Crown Center came into view, brilliantly illuminated, with more than fifty-thousand sparkling lights, its centerpiece, the one hundred foot tall Mayor's Christmas tree, adorned with over seven thousand lights and one thousand ornaments. Trisha grew tense. She didn't have much time to say what had been troubling her for days. She screwed up her courage. "Lassiter?"

Saying his name drew his quick, sideways glance. "Yes?"

"This marriage thing is getting complicated," she said.

Crown Center's Christmas lighting made the flex of his jaw muscles easy to see. "I know." He glanced her way again. "I didn't anticipate all the—volunteer work."

From his tone she couldn't tell if he was scolding or commenting. Well, if he was scolding, it was too late to do anything about it. Besides, would she have done anything differently if she'd thought about how complicated the volunteering would make her life? *No!* They'd done some good, and Lassiter had felt the glow. She knew it even if he refused to admit it.

She looked out of the window at the ornamental trees lining the walkway, every branch dramatized with tiny, white lights. Trisha loved the festive beauty of Crown Center during the holidays, but right now even the elaborate, twinkling splendor of the place couldn't lift her spirits, so heavy with guilt. "What am I going to tell everybody when we start on our new Habitat For Humanity home this spring, when you're not there?"

His driving gloves squeaking against the leather steering wheel drew her gaze to his hands as he stretched them, then fisted them again. "We decided from the beginning we'd say it was a whirlwind romance. That our wild passion burned furiously, then as quickly, went cold." He glanced her way. "They'll understand."

She nodded. "I suppose."

He was quiet as he pulled up in front of the hotel. "Look, Trisha," he said, shifting the car into park. "I'm on vacation this week, so for a while, you can tell them I can't volunteer due to my work schedule." He stared out the windshield. "After that, make up whatever details you want."

She chewed her lower lip. That was a definite "Don't call us, we'll call you" goodbye. "Okay—sure."

"Let me know when they need paint and paint supplies."

She was surprised by the overture. "You mean—for the next house?"

He glanced at her, his expression somber. "And the next, for however long you're a volunteer."

One of the valet parking attendants opened her door for her so she didn't have time to reply, even if she'd had the words. "Oh—um…"

"Ma'am?" the attendant interrupted. "Allow me to assist you."

Reluctantly, she turned away to take the man's helping hand. She was so stunned by Lassiter's offer she could hardly think straight. A moment later, Lassiter's hand at her elbow roused her from her daze and she noticed they'd entered the hotel lobby. She faced him, so grateful she had trouble holding back tears. "Thank you."

He nodded, but didn't smile or glance her way. Why did she sense he was annoyed with himself for the gesture? "You don't have to do it, you know," she said. "Nobody will think less of you." They crossed the lobby with its extravagant holiday floral arrangements, gleaming marble floors, rich Persian rugs and cozy sitting areas. A wood-paneled alcove beyond, housed eight, golden-doored elevators. "Strange, I got the idea you liked volunteering," she murmured, watching his profile, his wrinkled brow. "I guess I was wrong."

He made no comment. The elevator doors opened and they stepped inside. Their ride to the sixtieth floor and the private New Year's Eve party was hushed and tense.

After stepping out into the foyer, Lassiter helped Trisha from her long, wool evening coat. While he checked it for her, she took an abundance of deep breaths, trying to prepare herself. Not only did she have the "blushing bride of Lassiter Dragan" charade to stress over, she was having second thoughts about the pink-gold metallic corset gown she'd chosen to wear. The strapless, floor length creation laced up the sides and front like Victorian underwear, pressing her breasts upward. With its décolleté neckline and body-hugging fit, the ultrachic frock was far from prim. She felt half naked.

Then there was the trillion dollar diamond choker shimmering about her neck, along with matching diamond earrings, so-called Christmas gifts from Lassiter. Crown Center's glittering splendor had nothing on her tonight. Nervous, she patted her hair, piled on top of her head. True to form, too many wisps had disobeyed her struggle to create a sedate coif, and strayed down her neck and danced contrarily around her face.

Lassiter took her hand in his, jarring her. She jumped. He must have felt it, because he gave her a look. "Calm down," he warned beneath his breath, though he smiled for public consumption. "You'll do fine."

His surprise reassurance mollified her somewhat after his sharp-edged command. But not by much. "Ordering me to calm down is like ordering me to levitate three inches off the floor,'' she whispered back, her tone every bit as sharp as his had been. ''Some things can't be bent to your will, no matter how rich and powerful you are.'' She smiled for show, too, though she was far from happy. Why did he have to look so scrumptious in his tux? Why did his silvery eyes draw her, make her breathless, even when narrowed in disapproval? ''Now I'm practically jumping out of my skin,'' she charged. ''Thanks a bunch!''

He offered her his arm, his grin charming, his eyes flashing. ''You're welcome, my sweet,'' he taunted. ''Shall we join the others?''

She had a strong urge to spin on her stiletto heels and stomp out, go home, change into jeans and a comfortable sweater, and dash to Kindra's house for the HFH party. She opened her mouth to tell him exactly that when a flash blinded her. ''Great shot,'' Reggie said. ''Glitterati out on the town. Now you two lovebirds enjoy. We'll make ourselves invisible.''

When the camera's flash cleared from Trisha's vision, Reggie and Jane stood before them, looking quite natural in formal clothes. Even Reggie-the-hippie—looked suave. With his hair swept back in a ponytail, he looked exotic, like an artist—which he was.

Jane looked especially attractive in an ankle-length, satin tube dress. Cut simply, with a rounded neckline and long sleeves, its classic, demure style and aquamarine color suited the young journalist's complexion as well as her subdued personality.

''You two have some fun,'' Lassiter said. ''Forget work. It's New Year's Eve.''

Reggie laughed his big, open laugh. ''No worries there. I'll take a few obligatory shots, then we'll ignore you with great gusto.'' Slinging an arm about Jane's shoulders, he said, ''Let's check out the hors d'oeuvre tables, good lookin'. I'm starved.''

Trisha watched Reggie and Jane enter the ballroom and quickly melt into a crowd of around a hundred party-goers. The ballroom was approximately the size of four conjoined tennis courts. Nature murals graced the walls between floor-to-ceiling windows. Even in the low, romantic lighting, the hardwood floor glistened.

Antique furniture dotted the interior, but Trisha guessed the dainty commodes, marble-topped tables and ornately carved chairs were for ornamentation and ambience rather than to be used. At the far end of the hall, a stage ran the entire width of the room. A small orchestra played softly while couples danced. Near the entrance, where Trisha and Lassiter stood, a long line of tables had been set up, their white cloths flowing all the way to the floor. Silver trays, tureens and warming plates, filled to overflowing with delicacies glistened in reflected light of ornate candelabras. For casual dining and visiting, several dozen tables for four had been set up near the food. A flickering candle amid an evergreen centerpiece graced each small table.

It was all terribly elegant. Trisha felt like Cinderella, except she was arriving on the arm of the handsome prince. The room disappeared as her thoughts turned inward. In a couple of days, Reggie and Jane would be gone and she would be reminded of the Cinderella scenario again—when the designer clothes, the diamonds, the mansion were only a memory.

But unlike Cinderella's happy ending, the handsome prince would *not* be obsessing over a glass slipper—or in her case, a pink-gold, metallic stiletto—and he would *not* be madly searching for his ladylove who lost it.

As Lassiter led her into the throng, she tried to shake off her melancholy. Her heart wasn't into celebrating. She'd agreed to this deal, her reward a fifty-thousand dollar loan, so she could start her business, build her dream. She must not get sappy and sad over the man who thought so little of human relationships that he would hire a wife, *quid pro quo,* his emotions safely locked away, untouched.

Lassiter's voice drew her back, just in time to catch the fact that he was introducing her to their host and hostess, a sixtyish couple by the name of Richmond. She smiled with difficulty. The Richmonds looked familiar, and she realized she'd seen their pictures gracing the society section of the newspaper over the years. They seemed nice, though they were so absorbed with greeting each new arrival, she and Lassiter had barely begun to chat before their attention was redirected to the next couple.

Trisha had known her world was so different from Lassiter's it might as well be on another planet, but not until stepping into the ballroom did that reality hit her hard.

As the last day of the year marched toward its final hour, they mixed and mingled. Trisha actually shook the hand of Missouri's governor, then Hollywood's most recent hunky heartthrob, visiting family for the holidays, even the Kansas City Chiefs' new quarterback golden boy.

She tried not to gush or appear overwhelmed by the political, entertainment and sports celebrities, but it wasn't easy. On the other hand, Lassiter moved with ease through this stratosphere of societal elite, visiting with the well-heeled celebs as though they were close, personal friends.

Trisha was surprised when she was included in conversations, that her opinions seemed to be taken seriously. Nobody's eyes glazed over when she spoke. Nobody sneered, snorted or laughed or looked at her like she was an idiot—not the governor, the mayor, the quarterback or any of their wives. After a while she found herself almost as relaxed as Lassiter. Almost. She had to admit these people were a lot more like regular human beings than the gods she'd visualized, hurling lightning bolts down from atop Mount Olympus.

Around ten o'clock, when Lassiter got caught up in a friendly political debate, right next to the food, Trisha decided to sample the delicacies. With a dessert plate in one hand, she moved along the smorgasbord at a leisurely pace, selecting a fresh fruit flan, several mini minted Greek meatballs, a pecan and honey tart, two sticky pork riblets flavored with a plum sauce, and a deep-fried cucumber, which, after tasting, she decided she could have lived without. Everything else was marvelous.

"Food good?"

She turned to see Lassiter. Unfortunately, she'd just popped a mini meatball in her mouth, so she nodded. Holding out her plate, she swallowed. "Try a pork riblet. They're amazing."

He shook his head. "Maybe later."

"If they're gone, don't blame me."

"I promise." His grin was charming, however counterfeit it might be. "Having fun?"

She smiled, surprised at herself that she could do it and really mean it. "Actually, I am, as strange as that may seem. Did you know the governor and his wife have two dogs, both are from rescue societies? And she's very interested in getting involved with Habitat For Humanity? So is the Chiefs' quarterback. He even said he thought he could get some of his pro football buddies involved. Can you just imagine a Habitat For Humanity house built by the Kansas City Chiefs?" She snapped her fingers. "Oh, that reminds me, I told the mayor's wife I'd get her the address for donations to the Kansas City feral cat spaying and neutering society. I need to write myself a note and this handbag is so tiny all I put in it was a handkerchief and a couple of safety pins. Do you have a scrap of paper and a pen?"

He watched her as though he was seeing a rather interesting new life form. With a low chuckle he shook his head. "I leave you alone for one minute and you're recruiting more volunteers."

"Look on the bright side. This time it's not you."

"Good point," he said, still grinning. Reaching inside his tux coat, he drew out a pen and a silver business card case, from which he extracted one of his cards. "Use the back of this for your note." He started to put the case back, then stopped, extracted another card and handed it to her. "You might need to write yourself another note."

"Good idea." She plucked it from his fingers. If he was teasing, she refused to take the bait. "I'll probably need it. Hold this, please." She lifted her dessert plate toward him. After he took it she made a circular motion. "Now, turn around."

"Why?"

"So I can use your back as a hard surface."

He seemed surprised by the request. Apparently not many people used him as a writing desk. "Sure."

When he was facing away, she placed his card against his back and scribbled her note.

"By the way, what are the safety pins for?" he asked.

"Just for emergencies. It's a girl thing."

"Oh?"

She grinned at his clueless response. He might be rich and powerful, but he knew nothing about the wisdom of safety pins in case of a broken strap, defective clasp or loose hem. "Okay," she said. "I'm done. Thanks."

He faced her, settling an arm about her shoulders. "If you can spare a minute from your recruiting, I'd like you to meet a client."

As he coaxed her through the throng, she slipped his pen and business cards into her envelope-size handbag. Her hands shook slightly. Having Lassiter's arm about her was not something she could take completely in her stride. "Why do you want me to meet a client?" It seemed to her the fewer people they lied to the better.

"Because he asked me if he could meet you."

She was surprised. "Why would any client of yours ask to meet me?"

"He's also a friend. He just said, 'Is that your wife?' and when I said yes, he asked for an introduction. My guess is, he enjoys meeting beautiful women. He's been married often enough."

She experienced a blow to her heart at his use of the word "beautiful." Her face felt flushed and she couldn't meet his eyes. "There's no need for sarcasm," she whispered.

He said nothing for a moment and she wondered what he was thinking. "I couldn't agree more," he finally said, sounding serious. Against her will, her heart soared. Lassiter's solemn compliment was more thrilling, more electrifying than the gushiest flattery could ever be. She peeked at his face to discover he was watching her, his gaze steady, irresistible. She bit her lip to keep herself from blurting something foolish that would annoy him and mortify her.

"Well, well, Gent, old man," came a gravely male voice. "Who is this glittering peach you married, and why have you been keeping her a secret?"

That voice! Trisha would never forget that voice! Her gaze shot to the man who'd spoken. He was paunchier than she remembered, and had a lot less hair, but there was no question about his identity. He was the man who'd walked out on her and her mother twenty years ago. *"Father!"* All the old bitterness and anger came flooding back. She had trouble breathing and her face flamed.

She felt violated, betrayed. How dare Lassiter Dragan call such a thoughtless, selfish egomaniac his *friend?* Her anger billowing to a scalding fury, she spun on Lassiter. "I should have known you would be friends with—with *him!*"

CHAPTER FOURTEEN

LASSITER managed to remove his furious bride from the awkward situation with hardly a curious glance from surrounding partiers. Clasping her to his side in a vise grip he maneuvered her to the dance floor. "How was I to know Sawyer Henderson was your father?" he asked. "Fathers and daughters usually share a last name."

"I told you. Mother and I took her maiden name after the divorce."

"I'm sorry. I don't recall," he said.

"Why should you?" she retorted. "I'm hardly a flutter on your Richter scale. Like today's stock quotes, I'm useful for the moment, meaningless tomorrow."

He didn't appreciate her flippancy, though he had to admit that early on she'd been little more to him than background noise. He wished he still felt that way. "Did you tell me his name?"

"No. I prefer not to mention it," she said. "Besides, how was I to know you two were such buddies?"

She had a point. But calling Sawyer Henderson his buddy was overstating their relationship. "He's not a bad person, Trisha," Lassiter said.

"Ha!"

"I'm sure you have good reason to be angry, but the man's not evil incarnate." He released his controlling grip on her shoulders and turned her into his arms, deciding they could do a better job assuring their argument continued in whispers if they were face-to-face and close together.

"I don't care to discuss him." Her stiff body language told him she was furious enough to dump their whole deal and walk out. He couldn't allow it. The holidays were almost over. He wasn't going to let her blow their cover now, not after all

150

he'd done to assure himself the magazine article would bring him millions in new business and the bare minimum grief to his private life.

"Trisha," he said quietly but sternly. "Listen to me. You see Sawyer Henderson through the eyes of an eight-year-old whose daddy abandoned her and made her mother cry."

"Wrong!" she shot back. "Leaving us was the greatest thing he ever did. It was the eight years before that I can't forgive. He was a tyrant. He found fault with everything. He didn't believe in helping those less fortunate, and he cared more about making money than his own family."

"Okay, I'll grant you the man's far from perfect," Lassiter said. "But the Sawyer Henderson I know is nothing more sinister than a compulsive worrier. He agonizes over everything to the point where he wears out friendships, loses wives, ruins his health. He's more pitiable than he is detestable. Try to see him through the eyes of an adult."

She blinked, then shifted her gaze to his face. She still frowned, but she was listening. His smile was halfhearted, displaying his pity for Sawyer. "He's not happy, Trisha. I don't think he has it in him to be. He's become a business success, true, but it doesn't satisfy him."

Lassiter indicated the direction they'd come from. "Hell, he's on wife number four. Granted, she's twenty and attractive, but she's an air-head whose main focus in life is to drain him of his money for European trips and expensive jewelry. She'll soon tire of his complaining and worrying, and all the jewels and globe-trotting won't keep her from becoming the fourth ex-Mrs. Henderson. To be frank, under that jovial party facade you saw, he's a sad, frightened human being."

She lifted her chin, showing her defiance, but a pensive shimmer in the shadow of her eyes suggested that she might be seeing her father as a man, with flaws, yes, but a man who was less evil than pathetic.

"Sawyer and I have done business together over the years," he went on, "I admire his keen business sense, so I give him the approval he craves, in part out of respect and in part because I know he doesn't have the capacity to enjoy his success.'' Spreading his fingers at her back, Lassiter drew her closer. There was no real need, since their whispers couldn't be heard by nearby dancers. He simply couldn't help himself. "Sawyer worries every decision he makes is wrong," he said. "…that catastrophe waits around every corner, that tomorrow he'll be penniless. No matter how successful he is or becomes, he can't appreciate it because at heart he's a pathological pessimist.''

Lassiter dipped his head close to her ear, inhaling her light, seductive scent. "You couldn't wish your father into a deeper hell than he's dug for himself." As he spoke, he grazed her ear with his lips, hoping it was an accident. He was still irritated with himself for last night's impromptu kiss on her nose. "For your own sake, Trisha, let go of the hate.''

She shifted away from his touch to stare at him, her face tense, eyes swimming with tears. "That's quite a speech," she retorted in a quivery whisper. "So full of wisdom and compassion." She paused for a beat, and he sensed she was struggling to remain poised. "Just who are you and what have you done with Lassiter Dragan?''

He would have thought she was joking except for her pinched expression. He'd believed he was getting through to her, but her glimmering eyes told him all he'd done was make her feel betrayed. "What do you mean?" he asked.

"I mean, your insights into my father seem to be the outpouring of actual emotion. It's ironic that you feel sympathy for *that* man—of all people—but not empathy. Surely you recognize a connection, see parallels between yourself and my father!" she charged. "Or do you think you're so different, less pathetic, because you luxuriate in your wealth, never second guess your decisions and don't marry the women you— you *date?*" Her last word was spoken with such vehemence, it sounded obscene. "Does the fact that you find no value in family make you better than my father, or just colder?''

A lone tear slid down her cheek and he cursed himself for provoking it. He should have known she wasn't ready to hear any defense of the man she'd loathed most of her life. Words failed him as he watched her, suffering so acutely that even the proud lift of her chin and her squared shoulders couldn't disguise the emotional havoc he'd wreaked. He could feel it as they danced, in the rigidity of her spine, the inflexibility of her arms, the formality of her posture. Her cheeks were wet with tears; her lips trembled.

Silently witnessing her struggle, he bit off a curse, despising himself for causing her pain. He didn't want that at all. He wanted her to flow into him, wanted them to melt together. He longed for her to be soft and willing, with a totally different emotion shining in her eyes.

Did she have any idea how beautiful she was, even so furious and hostile she wanted to spit in his eye? Could she even fathom that all evening, as she'd stood by his side, his mind had only been partly aware of whatever conversation he was having with another guest, while the rest focused tightly on her every move, every word?

He knew each time she smiled, even when he wasn't facing her. He knew because whoever she smiled at lit up like a Christmas tree. She had magic inside her that drew people. Nobody on earth could prove that better than he. She'd cast her spell on him that day in the coffee shop when he scribbled the note on the napkin, and again when she walked into his office and he'd proposed their outlandish bargain—which hadn't seemed outlandish at the time. The irony was, he didn't do outlandish things, which only confirmed the erotic power of her voodoo.

He saw Reggie and Jane threading their way through the dancers and sensed another magazine moment on the horizon. "Buck up," he whispered. "I think we're about to have our picture taken."

"Oh, no!" Trisha slid her hand from his shoulder and swiped at her cheeks. "I'm not in the mood."

He felt the slap of her meaning—being held in his arms was not a mood lifting experience for her. "*Get* in, darling." He grinned at the approaching couple. "Hi," he said. "Enjoying yourselves?"

Reggie wasn't wearing his usual genial expression. In fact he looked rather conspiratorial. "Yeah, great time." He leaned closer to the couple. "Okay, I know it's not midnight yet, but Janie and I are heading out early, so we need the New Year's Eve kiss now." He lifted his camera to his face. "Let's have a soul-melting lip-lock for our readers."

Lassiter didn't know how soul-melting their kiss would be, considering he felt like a snake and he knew Trisha couldn't agree more. He was afraid this bow to tradition would be a fiasco that couldn't fool the camera lens. "Right." Trisha had put on her party smile, so he focused on her eyes, the only portal to truth. She was not happy.

"I'll take shots from several angles," Reggie said, "then it's *adios amigos!*"

Lowering his face to Trisha's, Lassiter threw out telepathically, *Just take the blasted picture and go!*

The initial touch of her lips was a jolt to his senses—disturbingly delicious. Lassiter's dour mood had left him ill-prepared for the hot thrill of their connection. His reaction was instantaneous, explosive, throwing him mentally off balance. With his mouth covering hers, he was privy to the anguished tremor lingering there. It was a poignant reminder that the kiss they shared was a lie—a tragic, bitter lie.

His lie, born of *his* lust, *his* greed.

But lie or no lie, and lust and greed be damned, he reeled in response. A detonation in his gut sent fire through his veins. He tasted her with his tongue, wishing he could lower her to his bed. He longed to slowly, lovingly undress her, to run his hands across her silken stomach, kiss her breasts. He wanted to whisper sweet promises to every part of her body, to seek out intimate pleasure points with his lips and his hands, to make her cry out his name on passion-swollen lips. He wanted—

Reggie's wicked laughter broke through Lassiter's white-hot cravings. "Whoa! This is a *family* magazine!" the photographer wisecracked. "Come up for air already!"

Lassiter held Trisha hard against him, wrapped in his arms as though the concept of releasing her was unthinkable. He became aware that she clung to him, too, their bodies provocatively melded. His breathing was labored, his throat dry. He met Trisha's gaze, saw the hurt swimming there and felt gut-punched. "I thought you were going," he growled at Reggie, unable to tear his gaze from Trisha's eyes. "So go."

Reggie's laugh rose up, loud and clear, over the band's soft, sexy music and the tittering of nearby couples who'd stopped dancing to watch. "I'm gone," Reggie said, with a knowing chortle. "But not as gone as you are, man."

New Year's Day began with a farewell brunch for Reggie and Jane. Though the food looked delicious, Trisha hardly tasted it. Lingering over coffee, the magazine couple shared the news that they were engaged. Trisha was delighted and hugged them hard, wishing them all the happiness in the world.

After a few, final photos, they clustered at the front door. Jane kissed Trisha on the cheek. "You know," she said in her whispery way, "Reggie and I have never felt close to our assignments, until you two." She blushed, smiling at them. "I hope you'll consider us friends."

Trisha was touched. "Of course. We matchmakers are very possessive."

She hugged them both and was amused when Reggie gave Lassiter a big bear hug, saying, "I never had a brother, man, but if I got to choose…" He released Lassiter and stepped back, for the first time seeming to be at a loss for words.

Lassiter smiled. "Me neither. And I would be honored."

Trisha had the oddest feeling he meant it. Fighting tears, she and Lassiter waved goodbye from the open doorway as Reggie and Jane climbed into Lassiter's limo for the ride to the airport. Standing at the entry of Lassiter's mansion, with his arm about her, didn't help banish her melancholy mood. Within the hour she would be heading back to her old life. She'd made a decision last night, and now was the time to tell him—before she lost her nerve.

When he closed the door and walked with her into the great room, she wondered if he realized his arm was still around her shoulders. He seemed preoccupied, so he probably didn't. Finding his nearness too stimulating, too troubling, she slipped from his grasp. They were alone for the moment, so she heaved a deep breath and faced him. "Lassiter, I've decided I can't accept your fifty-thousand dollar loan."

He hadn't been smiling before, but now his pensive expression darkened into a frown. "What? But—"

"Don't worry," she cut in. "I'll sign the annulment papers. I'm not holding you up for alimony or anything, if that's what you think."

"I wasn't thinking anything of the kind," he said, looking perplexed. "Why are you refusing the loan—after everything you've been through?"

She clasped her hands in a knot to keep them from shaking. "I just can't," she said. "No more than I could borrow it from my father."

"Your father?" He shook his head as though she wasn't making sense. "I don't see—"

"It doesn't matter whether you see or not," she interrupted. "I don't think you could understand if I stood here and explained for a million years." If she were to be totally honest, she wasn't sure she could unravel it for herself, even if she tried for a million years. She only knew she felt dirty and wanted out.

She'd never been a phony, a cheat, but she'd spent almost two weeks misrepresenting herself to a perfectly delightful couple and a national magazine, not to mention friends, Lassiter's executives and their wives, plus much of Kansas City's social set. She'd felt obligated to keep her word, but now that it was finished, her obligation was finished, too. "I know I'm giving up my dream—at least for the foreseeable future—but it can't be helped. I don't like what you stand for, Lassiter. It's that simple."

He made no show of anger, except in his eyes, which she had learned to read all too well. "What I stand for?" he repeated.

"You're a cold, calculating, money worshiping man. Oh, sure, you donate to good causes, but not for the right reasons. They're civic duties to you. Tax write-offs. You don't really care, not deep in your heart." She felt a surge of crushing sadness and imposed iron control over herself. She would not cry! "I hoped I could help you change your priorities, that by volunteering you'd learn to feel the glow. And you did, I think you really did, for a little while. But—but you froze up, again. I can't in good conscience accept your help. It would be like betraying all I stand for." She swallowed a threatening sob. "I'm going upstairs to pack. Please don't see me off." She turned and walked away, knowing she would never see Lassiter Dragan again.

Trisha was gone. Lassiter honored her request and remained ensconced in the den until she was well away. A week passed, then another. All the while he couldn't shake a nagging discontent. She'd done everything he'd asked, including signing the annulment papers. He chose to believe his restlessness was because he didn't like having his books unbalanced, hated being indebted to anyone. He owed her a great debt, and he wasn't happy about it.

In his business dealings, he passed Ed's Java Joint several times a week, and wondered if Trisha was there. When she'd left that job before Christmas, she'd assumed she was about to open her own business. Had Ed taken her back? Did she have another job? Was she out of work? He'd dialed her home number several times, but each time hung up before it rang.

More than once, he'd looked up Ed's Java Joint's phone number and each time glared at it for upward of an hour before he slammed the directory closed. What in blazes difference did it make to him whether she had a job or not? It had been her choice to refuse his loan. Let her deal with her decision. It was none of his business.

She was out of his life.

When January was half gone, on impulse he told his driver to pull over in front of Ed's. Snow fell, reminding him of the other winter afternoon, when he'd chanced upon Trisha in this coffee shop. This time, when he walked through the door, there she was. He knew her, even with her back turned.

Her friendly "May I help you?" died on her lips, along with her smile, when she saw who stood there.

Lassiter was amazed by how nice it was simply to hear her voice. He found himself smiling. "So you got your job back."

Surprise siphoned the blood from her face. She was pale, but so beautiful.

"The nephew didn't work out?"

She opened her mouth then seemed to decide against speaking. After a second she shook her head. He took that as a no. "I'm sure Ed's glad to have you back."

She ran her tongue over her lips. He knew it wasn't meant to be a come-on, but it was cruel, nevertheless. When she didn't respond, he said, "I thought I'd get a cup of coffee." Indicating the snowfall, he added, "It's cold." *It's cold?* Could he have said anything *more* stupid? What an idiot he was! Where had the glib, nonchalant Lassiter Dragan gone?

She blinked, but otherwise didn't move.

"Medium?" he coaxed, taking her in like a starving dog tasting his first morsel of food in forever. Even wearing that gawd-awful uniform, she was the most agreeable vision he'd seen in too damn long.

She blinked again, nodded vaguely, disjointedly, as though coming out of shock. "Oh—yes." She turned away. When she broke eye contact and presented her back to him, he realized he hadn't been breathing. How odd. He inhaled. Though his initial decision to stop had been impulsive, now that he'd found her, he knew his subconscious had been formulating a plan to balance the books between them.

When she returned to the counter, she held a medium size paper cup with a lid on it. He thought of the last time he'd bought coffee there, and of the vacuous assistant wielding a mop who'd caused Trisha to douse him with coffee. "I see you're not taking any chances." He lifted the cup from her hand.

"I try not to make the same mistake twice," she said, her expression somber.

The undercurrent of tension prickled over his flesh on spidery feet. She wasn't talking about coffee. She was talking about him. To her, he was a mistake she'd made. The thought tasted like gall in the back of his throat. "Right." He shook it off, raising the cup to indicate it. "How much?"

"Three ninety-nine."

He set the coffee on the countertop and unbuttoned his overcoat. "Trisha," he said, drawing his wallet from inside his suit coat. "I'm not here just for coffee."

Her attention was riveted on his paper cup, her hands flat on the counter. "We have excellent desserts. I recommend the toffee-fudge brownie cake."

"I don't mean that." He drew four singles from his wallet. "I think you know it."

Her gaze flew to his, then as quickly returned to the cup of coffee. "Our soup of the day is potato-leek."

"Look at me," he said.

Her only reaction to his stern tone was a slight flinch. She didn't look up.

He cursed himself. Who did he think he was, ordering her around? She wasn't an incompetent employee in need of a dressing down. She was a woman to whom he owed a debt. He struggled with his temper, trying for an even, courteous tone. What happened to The Gentleman Dragon? "Please." He held out the money. "Forgive me for being brusque. I've been—a little out of sorts."

That was putting it mildly. Lately he'd had to use all his willpower not to rage and bellow at everyone. He was exhausted from the grim determination it took to continually tamp down his frustration and anger. Why was this stubborn, slip of a girl so—so disruptive to his peace of mind?

Why did she insist on staring at the blasted coffee cup? *Damnation!* Whether she looked at him or not, he would get this said. "I've decided to loan you the fifty-thousand—interest free." There, he'd said it. An interest free loan was nuts, but it would ease his frustration, absolutely settle the debt.

He waited, watching, trying to probe into her mind. He might be descended from Gypsy fortune-tellers, but his heritage was failing him badly. From the frown on her face, he had no idea what she was thinking. Was she too stunned to believe her good luck? Was she pondering the offer? Was she planning his murder?

After what seemed like a year, she lifted her gaze, her expression more puzzled than thrilled. "When you offered me the deal at prime, you said only Santa Claus could give me a better terms. What's changed?"

Furious with her for asking a question he didn't dare ask himself, he growled, "Do you want to start a business or don't you? Accept my offer, *blast it!*"

His words echoed in the empty shop, bouncing off the walls, bombarding her from all sides. *Do you want to start a business or don't you? Accept my offer, blast it!*

Seeing him again, out of the blue, had been like a miracle. But her heart quickly plummeted from the stratosphere into a bottomless pit of misery. She managed a sad smile at the irony of his command. Wonderful, giving qualities lurked deep inside Lassiter Dragan. But raised the way he was, he had never learned how to offer a person any gift greater than money—his personal god. She knew his proposal was extraordinarily generous, unheard of, really. But it wasn't the proposal she needed to hear.

Yes, the sad truth was, she had fallen in love with a man who would never understand that love and tenderness and caring were all *better* offers. He could never imagine that for the gift of his love alone—untainted by a cold-blooded drive for wealth and power—she would happily live with him in a tent. And she would happily work in a coffee shop for years and years to save for her dream. As long as she could share those years with a man who cared more about the welfare of God's creatures than he did for the almighty dollar.

She accepted the four bills he held out. "I'm sure you mean well, and I thank you for your offer." Tearing her gaze from the sharp angles and shadows of his face, she moved to the cash register. She needed distance from the erotic pull of his eyes and his scent. After depositing the money, she returned with his penny change, forcing herself to look at him. The effort tore at her heart. He was just as she remembered, just as he'd looked so many nights in her restless dreams—so tall, so princely, carrying himself with unstudied, masculine grace.

She held out the copper coin. "Goodbye, Lassiter." By some miracle, her voice and hand remained steady. She didn't show she was dying inside, knowing he was about to walk out of her life—again. The polite smile on her lips was the most convincing lie she'd ever told.

His eyes locked on hers, and she saw emotion stir in their depths. The silence grew heavy, the tension sparking and crackling like static electricity. He glanced at the penny, then returned his gaze to her face. Something almost accusatory flashed in his eyes. With a curt half nod, he turned on his heel and strode out the door. She followed him with her eyes, a tall, dark silhouette, impressive against the snowy backdrop. Too soon she lost sight of him in the developing storm.

Suddenly the shop seemed unbearably cold. The wind picked up, howling like a wounded wolf. Snow pelted the plate glass. She tried to breathe, tried to fill her lungs with air, but her chest hurt, as though an iron hand squeezed her heart.

CHAPTER FIFTEEN

LASSITER sat at his desk, restless and moody. He couldn't think of a single reason for his sour attitude. Business was fine, great, really. "Yeah," he muttered, tossing his pen down. "Peachy." He turned his executive chair to glare outside at the overcast sky, spitting snow. Would this confounded weather never clear? He felt like he'd been stumbling around in a tunnel for the past month.

His secretary buzzed and he shifted to touch the intercom button. "Yes, Cindy?"

"A package for you, Mr. Dragan. It says 'Urgent: Open immediately.'

"Open it, then." He didn't need these trivial interruptions. He had a bad mood to feed.

"It's marked personal, sir."

"Then, bring it in!" he said, sharply. He closed his eyes, mouthed a curse. His secretary didn't hire on to be a scapegoat for his displaced anger. "I'm sorry, Cindy," he said, without the edge. "Please, bring it in."

"Yes, sir."

His petite secretary entered his office carrying a square, gift-wrapped box the size of a computer monitor, topped with a big, blue bow. She held it gingerly, away from her body, as though it smelled.

"Is there something wrong?" He rose from his chair and rounded his desk to help. The box looked a little heavy to be carried easily at arm's length.

"It's making—noises." She looked worried. "But not like a bomb or anything."

He grinned, indulgently. Cindy tended to be dramatic at times. "I'm gratified to hear that."

He took the box, which didn't smell, but was definitely

making noises. Scratching noises. "What the...?" Returning to his desk, he set it down. The ribbon fell away with one pull. He noticed it was wrapped so that the top could be removed without tearing through the red and gold striped paper.

"Oh, the card!" Cindy drew a square, white envelope from a slash pocket in her full skirt and held it out.

He took it. On the front he read his name, the word "Personal" and "Urgent: Open immediately." The attractive, flowing script looked as though it had been written with a feminine hand. He pulled out the card. A picture of a floppy-eared puppy graced the front, its head and forepaws sticking out of a cowboy hat.

He opened the card, blank inside except for a note in the same feminine hand, that read, "Doggerel was abandoned by the side of a road. Trust me. You need each other. Try getting a diamond tie-tack to give you unconditional love." It was signed simply, "Trisha," with the P. S., "It's late, but this is my *real* Christmas gift to you."

"No way," he muttered, hoping he misunderstood the message. Dropping the card to the floor, he wheeled around to stare at the box, now making whimpering sounds. "She wouldn't." Yanking off the lid, he was astounded to see how wrong he was. *She had!*

Sitting there, on a blue, terry towel, was the ugliest, most pitiful looking puppy Lassiter had ever seen. It looked like a string bean with huge, floppy elephant ears, big feet and short, black-and-white splotched fur. An unfortunate genetic hodge-podge of homeliness, with large, beseeching brown eyes. It rose up on its hind legs, draping both forepaws over the edge of the box. Lifting its snout, it made a bid to be picked up with a singularly mournful whimper.

"Oh, what a sweetie," Cindy crooned, coming up beside Lassiter. He noticed she'd picked up the card, ever the dutiful secretary. "Its name is Doggerel?" she asked, patting its snout.

"I don't know," Lassiter said, staring with disbelief.

"That's what it says on the card." She lifted the gangly mongrel out of the box and cuddled it in her arms. "He's going to be big. Look at the size of those feet," she said, giggling as it licked her chin. "What a doll baby you are, Doggerel."

"You want it?" Lassiter asked. Clearly Trisha had some deep, dark agenda that involved touchy-feely emotionalism. He had no intention of taking the bait. And it was such homely bait.

"Oh, no, no, no," Cindy said with a laugh. "My condo is just big enough for me and my two cats." She held the skinny creature toward her boss. "Merry late Christmas."

He didn't reach for the thing. He just watched it as it watched him. Those big, droopy eyes blinked, and it made that gawd-awful whimpering sound again. "He's so sweet," Cindy said. "Some cruel, heartless swine left him out in the snow to freeze."

"Probably its mother," Lassiter muttered.

Cindy laughed, apparently assuming he was joking. "I've got to get back to my desk, sir. Here you go." She pressed the bag of bones into Lassiter's chest. He sensed she was letting go, so he reflexively raised his arms to spare it a plunge to the floor. "Bye-bye, Doggerel," Cindy sang as she moved away. "Happy New Year to you both."

Lassiter stared at the beast in his arms. It seemed curious about him, too, and watched him silently. No whining. A long, pink tongue lolled out one side of its mouth; it appeared to be smiling. "Oh, no you don't," he warned. "Don't get any ideas about spending long winter nights curled in front of my fireplace. Your fairy godmother has gone way over the line this time."

An hour later, daylight long gone, Lassiter stood in falling snow, under the glare of a high-wattage spotlight, at the top of the outdoor staircase that led to Trisha's garage apartment. Her so-called real Christmas gift crooked in one arm, he knocked on her door.

"Who is it?" she asked.

"What the hell did you think you were doing?" he demanded, by way of introduction.

A few seconds passed before she opened the door a crack and peered outside, her expression worried. "Oh, it's you."

"Of course, it's me," he said. "Or do you have a lot of people banging on your door demanding what the hell you think you're doing?"

"You're the first tonight."

"I'm astonished. Are you going to let me in?" He indicated the puppy. "It's cold, and your Christmas gift is shivering."

She looked at the puppy, her frown deepening. She met Lassiter's gaze again. "Just so we're clear, I have a no-return policy."

That's what you think! He opted not to say it aloud, since gaining access to her apartment was his goal.

"Did you hear me?" she asked.

"Yes, I did," he ground out. "May we come in?"

She opened the door and he stepped inside.

The one-room apartment was small and cozy. A double bed with an old, iron head and footboard dominated one end, a rainbow-hued patchwork quilt serving as its bedspread. Perrier was curled dead-center on the quilt. The little white fluff lifted her head for a moment, seemed to sense that Lassiter was no threat, and lay back down. Lassiter eyed the dog, exasperated by its nonchalance. Apparently both females in this apartment were delusional. He felt pretty threatening at the moment.

He shifted his gaze to the other end of the room. A tiny kitchen area filled up the far corner with a stove, a sink and a refrigerator that looked old enough to be an antique. Open shelves above the sink held neatly arranged plates and glassware. A window was set in the middle of the wall. A small, round table and four chairs took up the remainder of the space at that end.

In the center of the room, on the opposite wall, crouched an aqua colored sofa, far from new, but sturdy and serviceable. Above it hung the famous imitation Oriental rug Trisha had told him about. Two overstuffed chairs in a paisley fabric faced the sofa. A coffee table, made from a barrel cut in half, separated the chairs from the couch. Several small, framed photographs were displayed on the knee-high table. Though nothing looked new, everything was clean and neat.

"Would you like to sit?" she asked, walking to stand beside one of the overstuffed chairs. She wore faded jeans, a pink, body-hugging sweater, no shoes but heavy, gray socks. He wondered if she'd been curled on the sofa reading. An end table beside the couch, made from the other half of the barrel, held a white, ceramic lamp that was lit. Next to the lamp, a book lay facedown and open. "Can I get you some coffee?" she asked. "Or tea?"

"How about some potato-leek soup?" he quipped, trying to hold on to his annoyance. For some reason, in her serious, cautious presence, with her pleasant scent all around him, he was losing his edge.

"You think you're kidding," she said, gravely, "but Ed lets me keep leftovers. If you want soup, I have soup."

He shook his head and took a seat on the couch. When he released the dog, it immediately scampered back and forth across the cushions, sniffing the book, the lamp and a velour, lavender throw that looked as though it had been hurriedly tossed aside when Trisha answered the door. "I'm returning the dog," he said. "This afternoon—that was not funny."

She took a seat in the chair opposite him. "I told you, I have a no-return policy."

"Hang your no-return policy," he said. "You returned everything I gave you."

"That was all for show, and you know it. A lot of thought went into my decision to give you Doggerel." As if on cue, the mutt flopped down, plopping its head on Lassiter's thigh, causing him to jerk in surprise. He eyed the puppy, making itself comfortable on him as if he were part of the furniture.

She waved toward the dog. "Look at that. Animals have a sense about people. He already loves and trusts you."

Lassiter's attention shifted to Trisha. "He just wants to be warm."

"Don't be so cynical." Indicating the dog again, she smiled poignantly. "Look where your hand is."

He was startled to notice he'd placed it across Doggerel's thin back.

"You're already subconsciously protective of him," she said.

He frowned, lifting his hand and settling his arm across the top of the sofa. He would not prove her right because of some accidental gesture. "Don't be silly."

She heaved a sigh. "Look, Lassiter, Doggerel needs a home and you need to feel the glow."

Provoked by her infernal crypticness, he muttered, "Glow-schmow! I can't take care of a dog. I work all day."

"Excuse me?" She sat forward, her show of teeth incredulous rather than friendly. "You have a house full of servants. I'm sure Doggerel can survive until you get home, even though he'll only have ten or twelve butlers and maids catering to his every whim."

Lassiter wasn't pleased with her logic. "I've never had a blasted dog. I don't want a blasted dog."

"Oh, Lassiter, can't you understand I'm trying to help?" She sounded full of pity and sadness. "That little angel mutt will give you more happiness than all the money in the world—if you open yourself up to the possibilities."

"Me?" he demanded. "Why don't you open yourself up a little? I offered you a chance of a lifetime—to give you your dream, interest free. You turned me down flat."

"Why?" she asked. "Why did you do it?"

Her question caught him off guard. "Why?" he repeated. "Because I owe you." It sounded strangely flat, hollow to his ears, but it was all the explanation he had.

"Not interest free, you don't."

She was right. Their original deal at prime was an unheard-of bargain. So why had he insisted on loaning her the money, interest free? His robber baron parents must be whirling in their graves. "Because you went above and beyond, helping me for that article," he said. As soon as the words were out of his mouth, he knew that wasn't it, at least not all of it.

She sat back abruptly, as though she'd been slapped. For a long moment, she watched him, her eyes bright with moisture.

Impatient and frustrated, he demanded, "Well, why the hell do you think I did it?"

Across her lovely face, a bright flush raced like a fever. Her brows knit, then the frown dissolved. She sat up straighter, seeming determined to get something said. "Because…" She let the sentence dwindle away, then shook her head as though shaking off her hesitancy. "Because you love me," she said, in a whisper.

He stared, shaken to hear words spoken aloud that he'd buried in a deep, dark corner of his heart. He hadn't planned to fall in love, wasn't in the market for love. So it had to go away. He would make it go away.

"You don't want to be in love with me," she went on, as though reading his mind. A tear slid down her cheek. "You're Mr. Quid Pro Quo, desperate to balance your books so you can be rid of me."

Unnerved, he scowled at her, watched the tear slide to her chin, dangle there for a moment, then fall to her sweater. Another tear followed the first. She didn't move, hardly blinked, her eyes on his face.

What could he say? He couldn't deny the truth. He loved her. For weeks he'd fought to keep from admitting it to himself. Maybe he'd failed that, but he had *no* plans to admit it. He didn't need a dog, a glow, a woman, a magic wand, Santa Claus or any other fairy story bull to fulfill him. He was Lassiter Dragan—complete, whole, a self-contained success story.

With a great force of will, he met the heartbreaking vulnerability in her eyes with cool reserve.

Trisha sat in tense silence, observing the man she'd accused of loving her. Hearing her speak out loud her crazy, impossible longing, threw her into a state of chaotic shock, if there was such an emotion. If there hadn't been before, she invented it. She was appalled at herself, so mortified she wanted to tear her hair and beat her fists against the wall, screaming, so sad she wanted to curl in a ball and die. Though she managed to suppress the screaming, she couldn't hold back her tears.

Lassiter said nothing. He sat there scowling at her, jaw clenched, nostrils flaring. He looked too big for her sofa, even bigger because he was angry. He wore a burgundy V-neck sweater over a black turtleneck, black cord trousers and hiking boots. Dark hair mussed by the winter wind, gave him a charming, free-and-easy facade.

Dressed casually, with Doggerel's head in his lap, he didn't seem like a cold-as-ice CEO. He looked more like a—well, like a nice, everyday guy. The impression he presented, except for his furious expression, was every inch the Lassiter Dragan she knew he could be—but rejected utterly.

So there it was, the frigid stare, the silent scorn. A bitter wave of regret washed over her, cold as death. She felt sick, humiliated. She'd as much as begged Lassiter to love her. How could she have been so stupid, knowing him the way she did?

Suddenly, time seemed vacant, hollow, a yawning chasm of emptiness and isolation, as though from this moment on she would be marking it, not living it. Her mind sluggish, without hope, she did the hardest thing she'd ever done in her life. Rising, she walked around the small coffee table and held out her hand. "It seems we're always saying goodbye, Lassiter," she whispered, fearful speaking any louder would betray her heartbreak. "If you keep the puppy, I'll consider the debt paid."

He didn't immediately take her hand. Needing him gone, knowing it was only a matter of minutes before she broke down completely, she bent and grasped his fingers. "Please go." She tugged, coaxing him to his feet.

He took her cue and stood. She pulled from his touch and scooped up Doggerel, settling the pup in his arms. "I'll never know if you ditch the dog," she said, unable to make eye contact. "Do what you have to do." He didn't move, so she grasped his elbow, propelling him toward the exit. "Don't come again."

At the door, she couldn't help looking at his face. His mouth was set in a grim line, his gaze direct and disturbing. Something inside her chest clamped like a vise, squeezing, twisting.

"I'll keep the dog," he said.

She experienced a rush of thankfulness, his promise a tourniquet on the slow, painful bleed-out of her soul. "Thank you," she murmured in a trembly whisper. Opening the door, she focused on falling snow.

"It cost you fifty-thousand dollars and your dream," he ground out. "I hope it was worth it."

She managed to prod them outside, close and lock the door, before she slumped to the floor in a shattered heap.

CHAPTER SIXTEEN

LASSITER sat in his favorite easy chair reading the latest spy thriller, his feet propped on an ottoman. A fire blazed fragrantly in the hearth nearby. The only downside—he had no idea what the story was about. His mind kept drifting to Trisha. Damn him! He usually had masterful control over his emotions, so why couldn't he forget her and move on?

Something landed on his thigh. He shifted his attention to see Doggerel, the pup's oversize forepaws on his leg, apparently in a bid for attention.

"What do you want?" he asked, sharply. "Don't I have enough trouble without you bothering me?"

The puppy reacted to his harsh tone by leaping away and hiding under his coffee table. He watched it go, scowling. It hunkered there, only its forepaws, snout and big, serious eyes visible. "What's that all about, mutt?"

Lassiter heard a throat being cleared from somewhere near the room's door. He shifted to see Marvin. "Yes?"

The white-haired butler approached. "If I might make a suggestion, sir?"

"What is it Marvin?" he asked, laying his book aside.

"It's about the dog, sir."

"The dog?"

"It's just that Mrs. Dragan and I had quite an interesting chat one day—about rescued animals."

"Don't call her Mrs. Dragan. She's not Mrs. Dragan," Lassiter said, though that wasn't totally true. He'd been very busy and hadn't quite gotten around to…well, he'd been busy. "What about the dog?"

"Well, Mrs.—rather, Miss Trisha told me that it's possible, if an animal has been mistreated, he might be frightened of loud voices, since he may have been yelled at and—and possibly hit.''

"Hit?'' Lassiter frowned. The idea of somebody striking such a little, harmless creature like Doggerel came as a shock. Of course, he knew about animal abuse. It was tragic, and people who abused animals should be whipped themselves, but he'd never thought of abuse in connection with this puppy.

He eyed the dog, cowering beneath the table, its big, fearful eyes pleading for love, or at least not to be dealt a blow. Good Lord! Suddenly he felt like the world's biggest rat. "Hell,'' he muttered, rising from the chair. Dropping to his knees, he lowered himself to his belly so that he could meet Doggerel at eye level. "Hey there, sport,'' he said quietly. "I didn't know about…sorry, okay?''

"Sir, you might want to slowly offer him your hand, palm down. Let him sniff you, then gently pat him.''

"Right. Good idea.'' He slid his hand beneath the table. "We don't hit in this household, sport. I'm sorry about yelling at you. It won't happen again.'' He had a feeling he owed a lot of *people* the same apology.

The dog unhesitatingly licked Lassiter knuckles and he felt oddly elated. "Hey, kid, you're pretty forgiving.'' He looked up at his servant. "Thank you, Marvin.''

The elderly man smiled. "You're quite welcome, sir. Is there anything else I can do?''

Lassiter returned his attention to the puppy and frowned in thought. "Did Trisha suggest how I might coax him out from under the coffee table?''

"I think you could pick him up, sir.''

"That sounds logical.'' He encircled the pup with an arm. "Come on, sport. We don't cower in this house, either.''

Scooping up the dog, he rose with it in the crook of his arm. "What do you think I should do now? I mean, how does one apologize to a dog?'' He felt a little foolish, but only a little. Sure he could make multimillion dollar deals, but he'd never had a pet. There was no shame in admitting he had things to learn.

"I don't know, sir." The servant indicated the chair. "Perhaps he would enjoy sitting in your lap while you read."

"Oh?"

"On the other hand, I believe there is a school of thought that would argue allowing the dog on furniture would be spoiling the animal."

"Yes, I can see that." Massaging the puppy behind his floppy ears, Lassiter gave the problem some thought. "What do you think Trisha would say?"

Marvin grinned, clearly pleased he cared enough to consider her opinion. Lassiter experienced a stab of bitterness and grief. Damnation! He had no idea where that question had come from. He told himself it wasn't that he cared particularly. Trisha was the only animal person he knew. And she'd given up one hell of a lot for the little guy. Whether he cared or not was irrelevant. It was only fair that he respect her desires where the dog was concerned. "I think she would be pleased, sir," Marvin said, still wearing that annoying grin.

"Mmmm." He nodded, not doubting Marvin's assessment for a second. Moving to the chair he sat down, propped his feet on the ottoman and set the dog on his lap. "That's what we'll do." He watched Doggerel for his reaction. At first the puppy just stood there, looking at his master. When he sensed all was well, he turned in a circle, then settled down, laying his head on his master's chest.

Big, droopy eyes searched Lassiter's face for a long moment. Then he sighed. The little dog actually let out a long, audible sigh. Lassiter stared, feeling a strange tug in his chest. It was almost as though he'd just been promised love, loyalty, gratitude, encouragement and protection, all offered up in that one, single breath.

Very carefully, so as not to disturb his dog, he reached for the spy thriller and began to read, or at least to try. After a time, he glanced down at the puppy. Its eyes were closed. He was asleep.

Lassiter found himself smiling.

* * *

Trisha kept in touch with Jane, so she knew that not long after the couple turned in their story on Lassiter and Trisha they'd quit the magazine to follow their dreams—together. Reggie struck out to achieve his life-long desire to become a nature photographer. Traveling with him, Jane concentrated on writing her plays.

Trisha hadn't been able to keep the truth about her temporary marriage to Lassiter from Jane and Reggie for long. They had been very gracious, considering how they'd been used. Rightly or wrongly, they didn't pass the information along to their former employer. More sad than angry, they lamented how "perfect" they'd felt Trisha and Lassiter were together.

Their innocent remark was painful to hear and impossible to forget, because it was so true. If Lassiter could only understand that most marriages weren't the refrigerated variety of his parents. That human connections need not burn, like dry ice, with every contact. That hiding his emotions, freezing them, wasn't really living. But Lassiter couldn't see that. His history, his upbringing, was a heavy burden he couldn't cast off.

She prayed every night that, by keeping Doggerel, Lassiter might find some satisfaction, that he might experience a taste of all that could have been. She hoped the unconditional love and companionship of a dog could allow him to feel at least a modest glow, thaw out a corner of his heart. If that happened, it would be well worth the fifty-thousand dollar cost to her.

Valentine's Day dawned with Trisha and Perrier flying to the Adirondack Mountains in northeastern New York state. Her destination was a log chapel in the woods, where she would act as maid of honor at Reggie's and Jane's wedding. Trisha thought the quaint location sounded so romantic, a perfect setting for the unconventional pair to become man and wife.

The flight was smooth; the driver hired to transport her to the wedding met her as planned. The road trip gave Trisha plenty of time to think, since the driver responded to her queries in monosyllables, and the jazz he played on the Jeep's radio blared too loud for conversation.

For much of the thirty-five mile ride, they jounced along a one-lane, dirt road that lead through a snowy mountain wilderness of fields, gorges, forests, and streams. Trisha tried to concentrate on the scene outside, peaceful and becalmed, except for the occasional flitting and darting of black-capped chickadees. Lassiter's face kept looming in her thoughts, and she had to redouble her efforts to concentrate on the landscape. Thinking about him was too hard, hurt too much.

Winding their way beneath a heavy canopy of snow-mantled maples, beech and assorted evergreens, they finally arrived at the tiny log chapel. Just beyond a split rail fence, it sat in the center of a forest valley. Mountain peaks surrounded it on all sides. A frozen brook gleamed in the bright sunshine, an icy tableau sculpted by Old Man Winter.

The air was crisp and fresh, the quaint chapel and its surroundings clad in winter white. Though Reggie and Jane specified the attire would be casual, Trisha wanted to look her best and had splurged on a sporty wool camel trouser suit, a jade turtleneck sweater and camel ankle boots. The ensemble wasn't designer chic, but it was smart looking and nicely cut. Trisha felt it hit exactly the right note for a wedding in the woods.

Her driver opened her door for her. With Perrier in her arms she stepped out onto the snow-cleared, stone walkway that lead past two other four-wheel drive vehicles to the chapel. Tall, narrow stained glass windows were set in the logs on either side of a rustic, double-door entry.

The driver got back into the car and picked up a book. Apparently he'd been hired strictly to drive, not to witness the wedding. She stooped to set Perrier on the stone path. "It was very nice of Reggie and Jane to invite you, so be a good girl." Perrier cocked her little head as if to say, *When have I not been a good girl?*

Trisha patted her pet's fuzzy head. "Good point." Straightening, she steeled herself, determined to be one hundred percent happy. Unfortunately, seeing Reggie and Jane again would bring a deluge of memories rushing back—memories she'd been trying to bury for weeks. "Concentrate on their happiness!'' she mumbled under her breath. ''Block out everything else!''

She hurried along the walkway and up the wooden steps to the small porch, Perrier scampering behind her. When she reached for the handle, the door swung open as if by magic. ''Why, thank—'' When she saw who opened the door she froze, dumbfounded.

Lassiter Dragan!

He smiled at her and she experienced a lurch in her chest. He was so handsome, with his knife-sharp bone structure, magnetic eyes and strong, white teeth. Why must he look so marvelous, so fit, in his body-defining, white cable-knit sweater and gray cords? Against her will and her better judgment, her heart did a cartwheel of pure, unadulterated joy.

''Hello, Trisha,'' he said, his breath smoking in the nippy air. Though he'd said nothing more than hello and her name, the significance of those words seemed tremendous. Perhaps it was his voice, so rich and mellow, reminiscent of a bronze cathedral bell. Or maybe it was the simple fact that the words had been spoken by Lassiter Dragan that made them momentous.

She opened her mouth to respond but nothing came.

He took her arm, leading her inside. ''It's good to see you.''

It was paradise to see him. Once again, she tried for a response, any response, but nothing came. She nodded mutely, feeling like one of those dashboard toys with the wobbling heads. Why couldn't she talk? Lassiter's hand at her elbow was light, but the consequence was severe. Had his touch rendered her speechless?

They moved down a short aisle between four rows of empty, rough hewn pews. Only three other people occupied the chapel. On a slightly raised stage at the front, Reggie, Jane and a black robed clergyman waited. An arched, stained glass window behind the trio threw a rainbow of color across the wedding party.

Reggie and Jane smiled as she and Lassiter came down the aisle. The wedding couple looked more like lumberjacks than bride and groom. Both wore flannel shirts and jeans. Jane held greenery and flowers.

"I'm the best man," Lassiter said when they reached the front. "From your expression, I gather you didn't know."

She glanced his way. "You—you knew I was coming?" She was relieved to hear her voice.

"Yes," he said. "I asked."

"Oh?" She had a hard time thinking. Her flesh was hot where he held her arm. Her heart beat furiously.

"Hi, Trisha," Jane said, hugging her and kissing her cheek. "You look stunning."

"Thanks." Trisha knew the instant Lassiter released her arm and tried to tell herself the loss wasn't profound. She hugged Jane back, whispering, "You didn't tell me he was coming."

"Are you upset?" Jane whispered.

I'm beside myself with joy! she confessed inside her head. *Just the chance to see him again is the answer to so many prayers. It shouldn't be, but it is!* She forced herself to reply with less reckless euphoria. "No—no, I'm not upset."

Jane released her, handing her the smaller of two bouquets she held. "I thought the least we could do was provide our maid of honor with flowers."

"You paid for my airline ticket." Trisha accepted the charming bouquet made up of evergreens and a single, pink rose. "That was too generous."

"Oh, balderdash, woman," Reggie said, taking his turn at a hug. "We wouldn't have had it any other way!" After a brief, affectionate squeeze he let her go and beamed at her. "It's the least we could do for our matchmaker." He slung an arm about his bride-to-be. "If we can ever do anything for you, girl, we're there."

She smiled, overwhelmed. Her holiday marriage to Lassiter might have been a disaster for her, but meeting Reggie and Jane, helping set their romance in motion, made it worthwhile. "Thanks," she said. "That means a lot."

The ceremony began quickly, since Trisha's flight timetable and her work schedule were harsh dictators. Still, she was grateful for even this brief window of time, to be able to take part in Reggie's and Jane's wedding.

Holding her bouquet, Trisha stood behind Jane, Lassiter behind Reggie. They were too close. Their sleeves brushed. She could detect his scent, feel his heat. Though she struggled to concentrate on the happy couple, her heart heard the marriage vows with a passionate and fierce intensity. How ironic— standing so near Lassiter, listening to the same vows a Las Vegas minister had spoken, uniting her with The Gentleman Dragon in holy—if fleeting—wedlock. Her sense of déjà vu was almost too overwhelmingly sad to bear.

Lassiter was physically near. Yet, emotionally, he was a man alone, choosing isolation over human connections. She wanted to cry out, beg him to take her into his arms. She yearned for him to whisper against her lips that he was a changed man, that he loved her and wanted the same things out of life that she did—that the quest for money was a snare and a delusion, not the true path to happiness. But that was her crazy fantasy. Reality was far, far different.

Trapped in a love that could never be, she suffered the torment of his nearness, her throat aching with grief. On the outside, she maintained the guise of a poised maid of honor, her smile a brave lie.

"I now pronounce you man and wife," the clergyman said, and Trisha managed a genuine smile as the couple shared their wedding kiss.

Wiping away a tear, she gave them both a well-wishing hug. "So where are you off to for your honeymoon?"

"We've rented a cabin not far away." Jane hooked her arm around Trisha's. "I'll work on my play and Reggie will get marvelous winter photographs of the area. Then this spring and summer we'll rent a little place near the Grand Canyon."

"Oh, how exciting," Trisha said. "I see great things happening for you both." She tried not to notice Lassiter, but couldn't help it. Her peripheral vision kept him in sight. He moved to the first pew and bent down. She told herself she didn't care why. He was probably picking up a parka. It was foolish, but she cherished these moments near him. Everything he did took on staggering significance. She knew she would run them over and over in her head once she was gone, no matter how hard she tried not to. With great effort, she faced Jane squarely, which required turning far enough away from Lassiter so she couldn't see him at all.

"We'd love for you both to come to our cabin for dinner," Jane said. "It's the least we can do, after your long trip. We've hardly had any time to visit."

"I wish I could. I've missed you both so much, but the only flight out to Kansas City is at three o'clock." Trisha was heart-sick. She wanted to see Reggie and Jane, to sit and talk for hours. Though she tried not to think about it, the biggest trag-edy of the day was knowing that only moments from now she and Lassiter would once again go their separate ways. "Ed's expecting me first thing in the morning and if I miss the three o'clock flight—"

"I could give you a lift," Lassiter broke in, not far away. "I have a plane."

A wayward thrill swept through her, but she reined in her longings, working to remain rational. He was offering her a lift, not his undying love. Sucking in a breath for courage, she faced him. What she saw startled the wits out of her, along with any answer she'd begun to formulate. Lassiter held a dog in one arm. The animal looked familiar. "Doggerel?" The mutt had grown a lot in the past month, but she recognized him. "It *is* you!" She cupped the animal's sweet, droopy-eyed face between her hands. "I didn't know you were here!"

"He was taking a nap," Lassiter said. "We ran around in the snow playing Frisbee for about an hour before you got here." Lassiter affectionately scratched the dog between his ears. "This little speed demon could be the next world champ—if the exercise doesn't kill me first."

Trisha released the dog and lifted her gaze to Lassiter's. He watched her closely, his eyes gentler than she'd ever seen them.

"I thought you looked really great when I first saw you." She bit her tongue. Had she said that out loud?

His eyes twinkled, his lips curving in a smile that made her go all melty inside. "Is that what you thought?" he asked.

"Um, yes," she said lamely, backpedaling. "I recall, I—er—said to myself, 'He looks—healthy.'"

"Thank you." Lassiter set Doggerel on the pine plank floor. Perrier sashayed over to greet the puppy, her stubby tail wagging up a storm. Doggerel was twice her height and half again as long. For the week Trisha had fostered the pup before deciding to give it to Lassiter, Doggerel and Perrier had been almost the same size. The gangly mutt obviously remembered the white poodle-mix, since his whiplash tail beat a mile a minute. The two canine pals were glad to see each other. Trisha smiled at them, then transferred her smile to Lassiter, refusing to mask her happiness. "You played Frisbee with Doggerel?" This was unbelievable news.

He shrugged, his expression slightly embarrassed, a heart stirring sight. "I read somewhere that puppies need exercise."

She eyed him speculatively, but on the inside she sang and danced with joy. Her fifty-thousand dollar puppy was truly working its magic. "Oh, you read it somewhere, huh?" She cocked her head. "Where?"

"In a book."

"A book?" she asked. "Don't tell me you bought a book about dogs."

"Possibly," he said, then laughed, shaking his head. "Okay, okay, so you were right. Happy?"

She crossed her arms, watched him, amazed at the new ingredient she could see in his features, his voice, even his stance—a buoyancy of spirit. It radiated from him like heat from a blazing hearth. She nodded, responding with a minimal, "Um hum." She didn't dare say more, for fear too much of all she felt would come tumbling out.

He indicated the newlyweds, talking with the clergyman. "So what do you say to the lift? They'd love for you to stay." His expression was sincere, his eyes compelling. "So would I."

"Say, kids," Reggie cut in, "Reverend Palmer and Trisha's driver are neighbors, so we were wondering if you'd mind a

switch? Trisha could you let the Reverend go back in your car
and Lassiter, could you take Trisha to the airport?'' Reggie
held out his arms in a gesture of helplessness. ''Our car's full
of camera equipment and junk, and we haven't done all the
dinner shopping yet.''

Trisha would have given a lot to ride anywhere with
Lassiter, but she didn't feel she should respond, since it was
Lassiter who was being put out.

''Sure, no problem,'' Lassiter said, his eyes on her.
''Okay?''

It was so, so much more than okay! She nodded. ''F-Fine.''
She winced. Stuttering? First she couldn't talk at all, now he
had her stuttering?

Jane and Reggie gave her a goodbye hug and told Lassiter
they'd see him later. As the other two vehicles drove away,
Lassiter helped Trisha and Perrier into his four-wheel-drive
rental. The back seat had been put down to give Doggerel
room to roam. When Perrier seemed bent on communicating
with the puppy by clambering on Trisha's shoulder, she put
her in the back. ''I'm surprised they remember each other,''
she said, determined to make small talk. ''It's nice Perrier gets
along so well with Doggerel.''

''That little squirt thinks everybody's his buddy.'' Lassiter
laughed, the sound touching her deeply. ''He has the household staff eating out of his paw. I came home the other night
and found him sitting in one of the kitchen chairs wearing
André's chef's hat.''

''Oh—my,'' Trisha said with a giggle. ''I hope you got a
picture.''

''About twelve.''

''I have to have one, Lassiter.''

''It's a deal.'' He glanced her way as they meandered
through a dense wood, dark even at midday. His smile disappeared. ''On one condition.''

A flicker of uncertainty coursed through her. She didn't
know how to react, what to think. She didn't even want to
think, since all her thoughts centered around loving a man who
didn't want to love. Hope surged but she batted it down. *Don't*

go crazy, she counseled silently. *The condition is not going to be your promise to marry him!* "What—condition?" she asked warily.

He pulled onto the shoulder and parked. "Stay," he said, shifting to face her. "Fly back with me tonight."

It wasn't a marriage proposal, but it would give her more precious time with him. Did she dare? Sure, he seemed different, warmer, and he clearly loved Doggerel. But was it enough? Could she gamble even a few extra hours near him just because he'd shown an ability to bond with a dog? Or would giving in to her desire only mean more memories must be buried in a dark corner of her heart? Nervously, she moistened her dry lips. *You must be strong, Trisha. No matter how badly you want to be near him, don't do it to yourself.* "I—I don't think so, Lassiter. It's just that—"

"I heard you've had your father over for dinner," he cut in, startling her with the subject change. She didn't know why she felt embarrassed. Maybe it was that stiff-necked rant on New Year's Eve at Lassiter's defense of her father. She felt bad about her flare-up now, since it had been Lassiter's objective portrayal of her dad that started her thinking, rather rethinking, her attitude. Finally she could see him as a man, flawed, but human. "Well, you took Doggerel, so I decided I could bend a little, too."

"Sawyer is very happy about it," Lassiter said. "You've done him a great kindness, letting him back into your life."

She didn't know what to say. Flustered by his unexpected compliment, she remained mute.

"Since you won't stay, forgive me if I use this drive to catch you up on things."

"We're—not actually driving," she corrected, checking her watch. They had time, but sitting so near him was hard. She didn't shift to face him, fearing that would be a bad mistake. Knotting her hands in her lap, she peered at him with great misgivings.

"No, we're not." He leaned toward her. His silver eyes held an otherworldly radiance in the semidarkness. "I've started a new branch of my company, called Dreams, Inc.," he went on. "For people like you."

She stared, astonished by this turn of events. He was hopping from one surprising topic to another. Feeling off balance, she didn't know what to think, couldn't even be sure her brain wasn't misfiring. Maybe he was telling her they had a flat tire. She tried to concentrate.

"I'm offering low-rate loans for start-up capital for small businesses, to deserving people who can't get loans elsewhere." he said. "Modest dreams, like your dog grooming shop, are just as worthy as high-dollar ventures."

Was she really hearing him, or just wishing it so badly she was hallucinating?

"Because of you, I've initiated what I call 'Days of Caring,' he went on. "Employees are allocated a certain number of salaried days off per year to do hands-on charity work." The look on his face mingled eagerness and tenderness. His eyes shone. He was passionate about this. Trisha could see it, feel it in the deepest part of her.

Lassiter Dragan, man of passion! The sight mesmerized her.

"For the next Habitat For Humanity home, I've pledged all the lumber—and my own sweat equity." A melancholy frown dashed across his features. "Since I last saw you, I've had a lot of time to think—about family, home, and dreams."

"I—I can see that." She faced him in spite of her self-protective struggle to rein in her errant yearning. "You've done some wonderful things."

A soft curve touched his lips. "I'm glad you approve."

"Oh, I do," she said, earnestly. If it had been hard to keep from babbling out her love for him before, she didn't know how easy she'd had it. She bit her tongue to keep silent.

"Trisha," he whispered. "You've shown me that families need not be cold and distant like mine. Talking about your mother the way you did, taught me that a family might own nothing, but if they have love, that alone will sustain them through the worst times. You've made me see that a family—

a loving family—can be the most valuable and satisfying reward in life.''

His words affected her deeply, caused a lump in her throat. A warm glow infused her whole body. ''I—I'm glad I could—help.''

He smiled, and her pulse raced. ''You did. Very much. So I'd like to give you your real Christmas gift.''

''My—real...?'' The lump blocking her throat choked off the rest of her query.

He nodded. ''I have it for you now.''

She was confused, seeing no packages anywhere.

He took her hand in both of his and lifted it to his mouth, brushing her knuckles with his lips. ''I'm offering you my unconditional love,'' he murmured, meeting her gaze and holding it tenderly. ''A little dog taught me a lot on the subject.'' He turned her hand to kiss her palm. ''And so did an emerald-eyed do-gooder with an unnatural passion for Oriental rugs.''

She sat there stunned, hope surging, billowing, overflowing. He'd actually said the beautiful, sweet, astonishing words she'd desperately wanted to hear. Even so, she refused to allow herself to rejoice. ''You?'' she whispered. ''Unconditional love?'' She had to say it, no matter how painful it was to utter her skepticism aloud. ''How can you say such a thing, when only two months ago you told me you saw no value in family?''

He held her hand, gazed softly into her eyes. He wasn't angry, just solemn. ''Because of you—Trisha. Because you have powerful magic inside you that can turn an unashamedly confirmed ice cube into a boiling flood of emotions.''

He touched the skewed place on the bridge of her nose. ''That is the most infuriating little bump,'' he said with a wry grin. ''It drives me wild, makes me want to build houses for charity with one hand while I feed the needy with the other.'' He leaned down, and pressed a kiss on the imperfection. ''Lord help me if you ever break a leg,'' he whispered against her flesh. ''I'd probably have to donate my office building to some feral cat society.''

He moved slightly away. His eyes drank her up. "You should be saying 'I told you so,' since you knew I loved you that day in your apartment." He shook his head. "I knew it too, but stubborn ass that I am, it took me a while to understand that loving somebody might not be a bad thing."

Trisha couldn't believe this was happening, that she wouldn't wake up. She touched the place on her nose, the awful blemish he'd kissed so sweetly. His warmth lingered there. He was real, so couldn't that mean everything he said was real, too? Could such a miracle happen? She studied his face, feature by feature. The honesty in his eyes, his gentle smile, were pure—indisputable. This was no desperate dream, no wild fantasy. He meant every word. Lassiter Dragan was the changed man she'd longed for.

Like the turning of a page, Trisha was suddenly free to love this man—now completely alive, completely open-handed and fulfilled. She was free to adore him, heart and soul. A surge of exaltation heated her body and she smiled, whispering, "You feel the glow, don't you?"

Her question seemed to catch him off guard, because he laughed. "Yes—yes, my little romantic, I do." The vehicle was full of him, his stirring scent, his rich laughter. Her senses thrilled. He touched her chin, tilted her face upward, kissing her. "I have another confession."

"Oh?" Her head spun with the touch of his lips.

"I never finished the paperwork for our annulment, so I'm afraid we're still married."

She was stunned. "What?"

He nodded, his expression serious. "No matter how I tried, I couldn't make myself say goodbye to the woman who showed me how to find that elusive glow." His lips caressed hers. "...the woman who couldn't be bought—who gave me the gift of joy."

She tried to get her mind around what he was telling her, but his soft, feathery kisses were making it hard. She backed away. "We're—married?"

"Yes, Trisha," he said. "It was wrong of me not to follow through with our bargain. I tried, believe me, I tried. My only excuse is—I love you." His soft vow wrapped around her like a warm blanket. When she only stared, he closed the distance between them and kissed her, his lips stroking, his tongue teasing, exciting, he coaxed, "I don't blame you for being shocked, but please try to forgive me. I'm lost without you."

"Shocked?" The beautiful, remarkable truth finally penetrating, she took his face in her hands. "Yes, I'm shocked. But, forgive you? I'm—I'm so—so…" She shook her head in vain. There weren't words to describe how overwhelmed and deliriously happy she felt. "There's nothing to forgive, my darling. You see, I love you. I think I always have." She paused, scanned his face, saw the flash of relief in his eyes, so endearing. Lassiter Dragan's vulnerability laid bare before her was the greatest gift she had ever received. "Sweetheart, all I want in the world is to share your life, be the mother of your children." A worry intruded. "You do want children, don't you?"

"Oh, yes," he growled, sweeping her effortlessly onto his lap. "How about by next Christmas?"

"It's a start." She smiled shyly, feeling herself blush. *Children,* with Lassiter Dragan. It was all so new, so wondrously new. She could hardly believe they were truly married—*and planning their family!* It seemed miraculous, impossible dreams could come true, after all.

"You'll stay, then," he said.

"Of course, I'll stay."

He chuckled, and she felt its pleasant vibration in the deepest part of her. "This is a wild guess, but I have a feeling Reggie and Jane dabble a little in matchmaking, too."

She kissed his jaw, giddy with happiness. "Shame on them," she murmured against the slightly rough flesh, so warm and tempting.

"We'll scold them at dinner." He teased the shell of her ear with his lips, teeth and tongue, an erotically transporting experience.

"Absolutely," she breathed on a sigh.

"And you'll fly with me, tonight?"

Twining her arms around him, she clung, feeling revived, reborn, all the way to her soul. "We'll fly, my love. Oh—yes, we'll fly." She kissed each corner of his mouth, tempting and tantalizing with flicks of her tongue. "But must we wait?"

Forrester Square

LEGACIES. LIES. LOVE.

Award-winning author Day Leclaire
brings a highly emotional and
exciting reunion romance story to
Forrester Square *in December...*

KEEPING FAITH
by
Day Leclaire

Faith Marshall's dream of a "white-picket" life with
Ethan Dunn disappeared—along with her husband—
when she discovered that he was really a dangerous
mercenary. With Ethan missing in action, Faith found
herself alone, pregnant and struggling to survive.
Now, years later, Ethan turns up alive. Will a family
reunion be possible after so much deception?

Forrester Square...
Legacies. Lies. Love.

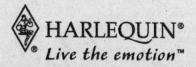

HARLEQUIN®
Live the emotion™

Visit us at www.forrestersquare.com   PHFS5

If you enjoyed what you just read,
then we've got an offer you can't resist!

Take 2 bestselling
love stories FREE!

Plus get a FREE surprise gift!

Clip this page and mail it to Harlequin Reader Service®

IN U.S.A.
3010 Walden Ave.
P.O. Box 1867
Buffalo, N.Y. 14240-1867

IN CANADA
P.O. Box 609
Fort Erie, Ontario
L2A 5X3

YES! Please send me 2 free Harlequin Romance® novels and my free surprise gift. After receiving them, if I don't wish to receive anymore, I can return the shipping statement marked cancel. If I don't cancel, I will receive 6 brand-new novels every month, before they're available in stores! In the U.S.A., bill me at the bargain price of $3.34 plus 25¢ shipping & handling per book and applicable sales tax, if any*. In Canada, bill me at the bargain price of $3.80 plus 25¢ shipping & handling per book and applicable taxes**. That's the complete price and a savings of 10% off the cover prices—what a great deal! I understand that accepting the 2 free books and gift places me under no obligation ever to buy any books. I can always return a shipment and cancel at any time. Even if I never buy another book from Harlequin, the 2 free books and gift are mine to keep forever.

186 HDN DNTX
386 HDN DNTY

Name	(PLEASE PRINT)
Address	Apt.#
City	State/Prov. Zip/Postal Code

* Terms and prices subject to change without notice. Sales tax applicable in N.Y.
** Canadian residents will be charged applicable provincial taxes and GST.
   All orders subject to approval. Offer limited to one per household and not valid to
   current Harlequin Romance® subscribers.
   ® are registered trademarks of Harlequin Enterprises Limited.

HROM02   ©2001 Harlequin Enterprises Limited

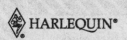

INTRIGUE

Nestled deep in the Cascade Mountains of Oregon, the close-knit community of Timber Falls is visited by evil. Could one of their own be lurking in the shadows...?

B.J. Daniels

takes you on a journey to the remote Northwest in a new series of books far removed from the fancy big city. Here, folks are down-to-earth, but some have a tendency toward trouble when the rainy season comes...and it's about to start pouring!

Look for

MOUNTAIN SHERIFF
December 2003
and
DAY OF RECKONING
March 2004

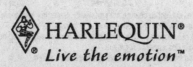

Visit us at www.eHarlequin.com   HICQMS

eHARLEQUIN.com

Your favorite authors are just a click away
at www.eHarlequin.com!

- Take our **Sister Author Quiz** and
  we'll match you up with the author
  most like you!

- Choose from over 500
  author **profiles!**

- Chat with your favorite authors
  on our **message boards.**

- Are you an author in the making?
  Get advice from published authors
  in **The Inside Scoop!**

- Get the latest on **author appearances**
  and tours!

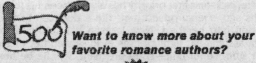

**Want to know more about your
favorite romance authors?**

Choose from over 500 author profiles!

**Learn about your favorite authors
in a fun, interactive setting—
visit www.eHarlequin.com today!**

INTAUTH

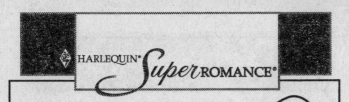

The Rancher's Bride
by Barbara McMahon
(Superromance #1179)

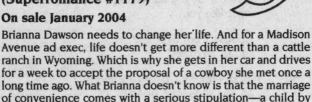

On sale January 2004

Brianna Dawson needs to change her life. And for a Madison Avenue ad exec, life doesn't get more different than a cattle ranch in Wyoming. Which is why she gets in her car and drives for a week to accept the proposal of a cowboy she met once a long time ago. What Brianna doesn't know is that the marriage of convenience comes with a serious stipulation—a child by the end of the year.

Getting Married Again
by Melinda Curtis
(Superromance #1187)

On sale February 2004

To Lexie, Jackson's first priority has always been his job. Eight months ago, she surprised him with a divorce—and a final invitation into her bed. Now Jackson has returned from a foreign assignment fighting fires in Russia and Lexie's got a bigger surprise for him—she's pregnant. Will he be here for her this time, just when she needs him the most?

Available wherever Harlequin books are sold.

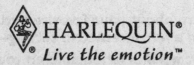

HARLEQUIN®
Live the emotion™

Visit us at www.eHarlequin.com   HSR9MLJ